The Defenestration of Bob T. Hash III

RANDOM HOUSE / NEW YORK

The Defenestration of Bob T. Hash III

[*a novel*]

DAVID DEANS

Published in the United States by Random House, an imprint of The Random House Publishing Group, a division of Random House, Inc., New York.

RANDOM HOUSE and colophon are registered trademarks of Random House, Inc.

LIBRARY OF CONGRESS CATALOGING-IN-PUBLICATION DATA
Deans, David
The defenestration of Bob T. Hash III: a novel/David Deans.
p. cm.
ISBN 978-1-4000-6700-8 (acid-free paper)
1. Title.
PR6054.E233D44 2008
823'.914—dc22 2007039972

Printed in the United States of America on acid-free paper

www.atrandom.com

2 4 6 8 9 7 5 3 1

Book design by Susan Turner

"There is in the world no rock or tower of such a height that it cannot be scaled by any man (provided he lack not feet)."

From *The Great Didactic* (1649) by J. A. COMENIUS,
author of *Orbis Sensualium Pictus* (1658)
and *The Gate of Tongues Unlocked* (tr. 1659)

The Defenestration of Bob T. Hash III

The only place where anything fun ever seems to happen in the Acme language course book *Forward with English!* is in the section known as Everyday Accidents and Domestic Mishaps. To illustrate what an everyday accident or domestic mishap might consist of, various familiar and generally very careful picture book characters volunteer themselves as the unwitting victims of a moment's dapper imprudence. We wince at the sight of a chin getting scratched by a razor in a bathroom mirror, we gasp at fingers straying too near the burner of a kitchen stove, we chuckle at the picture of a fedora hat (*Br. Eng.: "trilby"*) getting whisked off into a neighbor's hedge by a freak gust of wind; while the sight of a parrot suddenly turning into a man and falling off its perch will give many reason for pause. I think what makes those cheeky pastel-and-ink cartoons in the mishap section so interesting is that for a brief, tantalizing moment they offer the only clue that there might exist another dimension outside the world of scheduled routines and codified speech bubbles that reign elsewhere in *Forward with English!* Of course, by the Repairs and Rectifications section that follows, the regular world of clockwork expectations is securely back in place, if not *quite* quickly enough to have stopped us catching a glimpse of that other somewhat whacked-out dimension beyond. We are left now pondering a parallel world of heady misadventures and fabulous picaresques; a world where, time standing still—unchecked, benignly—events might one day run amok.

Actually, that last little inconvenience—the parrot turning into a man and falling from its perch—hasn't quite made it into the picture book yet (which is not to say that it won't appear in the forthcoming edition of the course, due out next fall). But otherwise, it was those vignettes of chin, fingers, and hat that flashed through my mind when, on the morning of Bob T. Hash III's madcap elopement, I found myself crashing toward the parquet tiles on his living room floor, parrot stand in tow.

In its career as parrot stand so far, the T-shaped branch of local elm wood (anchored vertically in a pail of cement, and to which cage, perch, mirror, and so forth were affixed) had, without ever toppling, survived numerous unintended knocks with caster-propelled items of interior furniture, been leaned on by umpteen tipsy houseguests, withstood a score of disoriented somnambulists, and brushed off sundry blitzkriegs of indoor Frisbee. Till that morning, however, its ability to support the weight of a fully grown adult human being attempting to balance himself on the extremity of one of its prongs had yet to be put to the test. When, mentally, I ran events backward and in slow-motion replay, I watched in fascinated horror as the parrot stand restored itself to the vertical, dragging in its wake an almost biblical multitude of birdseed that appeared to spring off the carpet—like a tiny tornado passing over a field of golden ripe wheat in *The Wizard of Oz*—to funnel itself, unspilled, back into the little seed trough. I watched an assortment of primary-colored plastic amusements from Astor's, the pet shop, hop, skip, and jump into the air and clip themselves trimly to the bars of the cage, which, itself having become detached on impact, had thrice cartwheeled across the living room floor.

For a few dazed moments, among a freshly laid bedlam of birdseed, I lay there flat on my back, staring at the ceiling in amazement. A halo of cartoon stars spinning round my head and a watery bird whistle twittering inside it, I found myself wondering how the picture book artist might try to depict my own misadventure for some future edition of *Forward with English!,* thereby admitting it too to that select pantheon of mishaps. In the "before" picture, for example, you could have an African gray parrot, sensibly perched at the living room window, with nothing, barring a wink, to suggest an impending disaster. Beside it, in the "after" vignette, you could then have a man in a suit—necktie floating into the air like in an astronaut's weightlessness experiment, businessman's glasses dancing off the bridge of his nose, staring at us with that look of mild astonishment, as if someone had just played a practical joke on the departmental manager by announcing an unexpected downturn in the quarterly sales figures while he was practicing on the office trampoline during lunch break.

So, mishaps occur. And yet, with a little more care, how easily disaster might often be averted: shaving more slowly, keeping one's eyes peeled for banana skins under a window—in my case, repairing to a more reliably solid piece of furniture the next time I'm about to switch from the psittacine form to the so-called *Homo sapiens.* The only other time this happened I also ended up stranded on the parquet floor of the Hashes' front living room. The main difference being that then, on my first metamorphosis, it was night, and the house was sound asleep. Another difference was that (purely by chance, having not the faintest inkling of the little miracle that was about to occur) I had happened to be stationed on a magazine rack—that is, one of several "low altitude" secondary perches positioned around the house for me to fly to. Under my newly acquired bulk on that occasion, the news rack simply toppled over onto its side—rather than crashing to its doom like the parrot stand was to do on my second transformation. One minute there I was, a parrot minding my own business, quietly perched on the magazine rack; the next, out of the blue, I was a fully grown man, platypussing about on the floor amid an assortment of back issues of the *Belmont Gazette* and the *Grammarian's Quarterly*!

My state of human-hood on that maiden transformation was to last just a couple of hours or so—long enough, nevertheless, to take a nocturnal spin in the family convertible, top down for the stars and the soft warm air of night. More to the point, it was long enough to give me a taste for the life lived by humans, as opposed to the life I had led as a parrot. Till that fateful night I'd been content with my lot. Of course, I'd heard lots of good things about being a human, don't get me wrong, many good things, but I had yet to be convinced. Did humans wink at little round mirrors, or ting little bells as often as I did? How often did the average human get the chance to imitate an interlocutor's question word for word in a loud, screechy parrot voice—to the delight of lady company especially? In short, why take the car when you can run up and down the little multicolored ladder? Of course, it might seem a little sweeping, a little bit reductive, to equate being human with driving an automobile, when you consider that even in our own picture book town of Belmont there are many other things besides driving a car that its inhabitants can do to show that they're human, and therefore many other ways I myself might have made use of my humanoid hours. But, let's face it, there were good reasons for my going for a spin in the car that night.

One reason was that my sudden, serendipitous possession of a cat burglar's arms and legs was perhaps a window of opportunity to do things not normally open to one in possession of mere talons and wings. While a variety of human gadgetry was already within my parrot's range (light switches, microwaves, I'd long ago mastered), a whole gamut of more sophisticated large-scale machines had till that moment been beyond my control. To coordinate at the same time, for example, not just a steering wheel but a gearshift and a set of pedals (not to mention a mirror or two) clearly requires the ability and reach of a full set of humanoid limbs. A second and perhaps even better reason was the avoidance of any potential alarm my newly acquired human form might give to an insomniac Hash, if one of them were struck by a midnight pang of hunger and came downstairs in their slippers to fetch a bowl of Froot Loops. All in all, it seemed a good idea to spend whatever man-hours I was going to get off the premises and away from the house.

I took to driving like a duck takes to water—no need for lessons! I just turned the key in the ignition—and with it the irrepressible dashboard audiocassette of *Forward with English!*: *"Taking a Trip in the Car."* I pulled out of the Hashes' white picket fence estate with all the graceful carbon-friendly tact of a milk cart. I drove through sleeping suburb till I reached Duck Pond, where suburb turned into field, with the volume down low.

Picturing myself as a very tall parrot in monocle and cravat on the turnpike for neighboring Bellville, I admired moon-lumined farmlands—fields of grain, a collection of cows, the odd *In Cold Blood*–ish barn.

Roadside signs and instructions were as helpful as the most limpid of phrase books from the Acme collection: *pass through flashing amber with caution—cry-wolf-ish spring-loaded antlers—snowflake.*

Presently, some ten miles short of Bellville, no doubt due to the meagre parrot proportions of my last meal being insufficient to supply my new, inflated humanoid energy needs, I began to feel rather peckish. So, when I saw the neon sign of an anonymous but conveniently located roadside diner, I decided to pull into its neat little car lot divested at that hour of patrons.

I strolled inside that diner like a John Wayne plonked on the moon; and I asked the nice waitress for a fish burger please. I leaned on the long zinc counter with tall toadstool stools and the waitress (presumably having recognized the trademark Bob T. Hash III Plymouth Fury as it swung into her empty car lot and jumped to conclusions)—when I asked her if she would mind putting it in a takeout receptacle—said *not to worry, Mr. Hash, you get a takeout box whether you stay inside the diner or eat it out in your car with the roof down open to the stars and the soft warm air of night.* It was not until some time later, to my own great shock and amazement, that her mistake made a great deal more sense.

Back in the car, under the stars, the burger turned out to be woefully short on the sesame front and, to be frank, was a great disappointment (*see* Lodging a Complaint, *Forward with English!*). I'm not eating at that place again, thank you very much. On the other hand, by sticking the drinks straw into the roof of the little carton, I was able to produce a crude sort of sailboat—which at least made up for not getting some wee free toy such as a hand-painted dragon-slaying medieval knight in armor or a bleeping limbo martian with irreplaceable batteries in the first place. Against the now setting moon, pendulous and yellow over a cornfield, sailed my little *Medusa* like a pedaling E.T., bobbing at the end of an outstretched wing (or, should I say, arm), its passengers doomed. Right then, as I was watching this, I got a funny sensation. It was a sixth sense, a kind of inner gas gauge, warning me that my trial stint as human was already nearing its end—and that it was perhaps now a very good idea to get myself, and Bob T. Hash III's Plymouth Fury, back to Belmont before this event actually happened.

The green grass joys of neighboring Bellville, where I've heard there's a mall, have to wait for another occasion. A wise twit-awoo perching in a tree watched me turn the car round in the burger lot—swiveling its head the way owls do to stare at my taillights—back toward the way I had come from. From the east the dark ink of the sky was already starting to drain and already I could make out the fond shadowed silhouette of Belmont. By the time Bob's alarm clock went off at a quarter to seven (unseen birds atwitter with song), the car had been returned undamaged to the pea-stone drive and I, once more an African gray parrot and picture book mascot, had been returned to my living room perch as if nothing had happened.

There is an order of things that happen to us (and I would obviously include my own species-flip in this category) that strike us as so monumental, so life altering—events that so change our outlook not simply on the correct use of the present perfect, say, or the pros and cons of bilabial fricatives, but on the very purpose of life itself, and we know that from that moment on our lives will never be the same. I knew then that, for me, from that day onward, trotting up and down little colored plastic ladders would never again hold *quite* the same appeal as it had done thitherto. Add to that the prosaic truth belying an impression of a supposedly adventurous, multithemed lifestyle, which might be gleaned from a cursory flick through the picture book where you can see me in a variety of vignetted locations. There I am, sitting on top of a filing cabinet in the office; there I am, blending into the exotic fruit wallpaper in the coffee shop (if rather monochromatically—I am not, repeat not, a macaw); and there I am again, perched on the shoulder of a peg-legged, patch-eyed pirate poised over a doubloon-filled chest exhumed on a coconut beach, a schooner anchored in the glistening bay behind me. But the truth is, I'm afraid, that 99 percent of the time I might as well have been glued to my living room perch by the talons.

That miraculous species-flip and run in the car, then, had brought home with sudden poignancy the limitations of a life spent sitting on perches and also, given the felicitous possibilities of creative composition, put into stark relief the absurdity of plucking mimicked fragments from a store of prefabricated phrases in the fashion of parrots. That flip transformation, so entirely unexpected, had offered, in tandem with the mishap page, a foretaste of another world—not just of the burger-munching rally driver, but the whole wild glittering tragedy of humanoid existence itself. From that moment on, up there on my perch, I began to daydream of leading a double, Jekyll-and-Hyde-type existence: mascot parrot by day, the thrills and spills of a tormented Hamlet by night. Having dipped my toes into the realm of the human, I could hardly now restrict myself to the same tired party tricks as before—like a sad Phil Silvers in his nursing home watching reruns of Sergeant Bilko.

By the way, for anyone unfamiliar with *Forward with En-*

glish! (seventh edition), this is probably a good moment to introduce the Family Hash *en famille,* as seen, in loco, on the lawn in front of their house—please look at page 2 of the companion picture book as you're reading this sentence. There, against the backdrop of the veranda, in his weekend cardigan, stands business tycoon and eponymous paterfamilias Mr. Bob T. Hash III. That charming creature beside him in a shinlength A-line pleated cotton skirt and sensible blouse is Matilda, his wife. Around them are gathered the picture book daughters Betsy, with hockey stick, and pigtailed Jane, leaning on her bicycle, and picture book son, rascal Bobby, freckled like the little boy on the cover of *Mad.*

Naturally, since it was probably a bad idea to repeat my astonishing transformation while the above described Hashes were up and about (*No, I don't think we have met before, actually*), I waited for night before making my first attempt to do so—which in any case, alas, proved a failure.

The TV off, the house gone quiet, I closed my eyes tightly, ruffled up my feathers, held shut a lungful of air, and, well, sort of squeezed as hard as I could—imagining that I could somehow transmute myself into a man by sheer willpower alone. I let out my breath and opened my eyes: in the little round mirror, attached on the outside to the bars of the cage, I confronted a rather sheepish and dimly lit reflection of an African gray parrot, perched and feathered as before. I did the special wink and tried it again: composing myself, shutting my eyes, inhaling another—if not the same—lungful of air, and squeezed even harder. But again to no avail.

The truth is that it is more difficult to flip from being a parrot to a man than it looks. Of course, not really knowing what on earth had brought that transformation about in the first place, I wasn't quite sure how I actually intended to repeat it. A little inventiveness was going to be key. The next night, for example, I tried flying round and round the living room airspace in a circle till it made me go dizzy. But that didn't work either.

The night after that I tried running up to the top of my ladder and giving the mirror a wink, then running back down, doing this over and over. Quite how that sort of thing was supposed to work I don't know but in any case there was again no result. The night after *that,* I tried secreting myself under a doily and reciting the well-loved enigma, *Who's a pretty Polly, who's a pretty Polly!* Once again, I remained firmly imprisoned within the genus of parrot.

As the week wore on it became apparent that my experiments were getting me nowhere and I not unnaturally began to grow discouraged. Perhaps I was deluding myself? Perhaps I would never again get the chance to be a human being? Perhaps I never *had* been a human being in the first place—and that ride in the car to the diner had only been a dream?

I was on the verge of giving up hope of ever resuming my admittedly very fledgling existence as a human being when, earlier on that morning of the thrice-cartwheeling birdcage, I happened to witness something that gave me fresh hope. The family breakfast was over. Matilda was clearing the table. Bob was upstairs digesting his Cheerios and packing his business trip suitcase. By hopping from one perch to another I could watch them in turn. Betsy and Jane, for example, now nourished by the goodness of Froot Loops and armed with hockey sticks, pigtails, and impeccable homework, had set off to the corner to wait for the yellow bus to come and take them to school. Bobby, the little rascal, was lagging behind—his satchel nowhere to be found—until I saw him running out to the car in the driveway: of course!—yesterday he'd not come home on the bus at all. He'd gotten a lift back in the car from junior baseball.

From my vantage point at the living room window, I watched him clamber into the back of the car and, seconds later, emerge triumphantly with the satchel aloft—in the process of which his feet just happened to scuff something out from the backseat and onto the pea stone. It was the partially crushed fish burger box the waitress had given me at the diner, with the cute little sailboat straw mast still in its roof. I knew then that my nocturnal humanoid joy ride had *not* just been a dream after all.

Bobby, satchel in hand, was by now trotting up Remington Drive to catch up with his sisters—oblivious of his role in uncovering the burger *Medusa* and in jolting my memory regarding the visit of the vet. Bob had meanwhile himself set off in a bright yellow taxi for Belmont International Airport for his business trip—more on that in a moment. That left just Matilda, my favorite. I watched her getting ready to head out for the shops: applying a light touch of mascara and then setting off down the porch steps, her heels receding from earshot.

One thing I'd not yet considered, in my somewhat ad hoc approach to discovering what had turned me from a parrot into a man, was the role that a visit from Dr. Horowitz, the picture book vet, may have played. It seems obvious now of course, but it wasn't till Bobby kicked out my now unmanned and slightly storm-damaged *Medusa* that I recalled it at all. I remembered how on the day preceding my first metamorphosis, Dr. Horowitz (half-moon glasses, stethoscope, and an identical twin to the picture book doctor) had paid a house call to our home on Remington Drive for a rigged-up picture book demonstration—with myself playing the role of patient, and Matilda acting as his assistant.

A feces sample, notwithstanding the rigged-up nature of the business, was collected by means of a spatula from the base of my cage and winged forth to a laboratory located on the far side of Belmont in the bowels of the veterinarian school for a follow-up analysis. But no need to wait for the results—this was psittacosis, announced Dr. Horowitz, "make no mistake!" And yet I had neither the shivering nor the rheumy eye discharge, nor the "fluffed-up scrubbiness" of the feathers, none of the horrible symptoms of that nasty dreaded disease. In fact, I was as fit as a fiddle. Nevertheless, up popped the gladstone bag, brimming with bottles and other weirdly shaped containers. Tablets were selected and ground into a powder with a mortar and pestle. To the pulverized pills was then added a mystery tincture from an unmarked blue glass vial (oxytetracycline?) that produced a crazy plume of purple smoke.

Like the model parrot, the loyal mascot, I had taken part in the demonstration in good faith. At the same time, I was watching the subsequent pharmacological preparations with a gathering sense of foreboding. On the vet's departure, a conscientious Matilda—as per Dr. Horowitz's instructions—had taken my cuttlebone and dipped it into the mortar, allowing it to absorb the pharmacological paste (a curl of wet icing sugar on the end of a rusk), which then was allowed to dry before being wedged back into the bars of my cage. Now, most likely the reason I'd not at first made the connection between Dr. Horowitz's visit and my extraordinary transformation later that night was, I now realized, because of the time lag between my ingestion of the concoction (via my brush-your-teeth-type sharpening scrape on the cuttlebone) and the kicking in of its actual effects. By the time the effects did kick in, when I fell off that magazine rack at a quarter to three in the morning, I'd long since forgotten about the events of the day before.

After my recent run of disappointments, I was excited by my new theory, and, prompted by the sight of my little carton *Medusa,* I was impatient to put it to the test. With Matilda gone I was once more alone—just me and the audiocassette of Everyday Accidents and Domestic Mishaps going round and round on the same bunch of everyday accidents and mishaps. I felt I could risk an experiment without needing to wait for nightfall. So I sidled along the elm branch toward the bars of the cage from which the cuttlebone protruded. (I should say that I rarely actually ever go inside the cage: it's really kept more as an accoutrement holder—for the ladder, the mirror, the seed tray—than as a cage per se.) For a few moments, I just stared at the cuttlebone, my head cocked over first to one side, now to the other, pondering its medicinal properties. Summoning up the courage, I leaned in toward it and scraped it with my bill. It made a rasping sound, like fingernails on a blackboard. I scraped some more to keep my bill sharp and true.

And, well, that seemed to be that: no fanfare, no stars and stripes belting into the wind. Ho hum, said I, and sidled back to my favorite section of the perch (a knot on the branch, which stops you from sliding round and hanging upside down like a bat). Here, I said to myself, I might wait at no loss of profit. And, bearing in mind the time lag between ingestion and kick-in from my first experience, I readied myself for the long haul. Might as well listen to the audiocassette of Everyday Accidents and Domestic Mishaps. Basically, it wasn't worth moving to a less precarious location (where the views are invariably inferior to those from less stable aeries) for a good couple of hours yet— or at least that's what I believed. What reason had I for thinking the magic transformation would this time happen so much more suddenly, so much sooner than last?

The whirling cartoon stars and bird whistle gone now, I picked myself up off the living room floor, brushed off birdseed that had embedded itself into my hands and feet, and blinked in sheer astonishment. Where a moment ago I'd had wings, I was now in possession of arms, and of feet where there once had been talons; for my bill I now had a nose and a mouth. I had a torso; I had elbows and knees. I had fingers and toes. And to top it all off, I was already fully decked out in a gentleman's suit.

But rather than dash off for another spin in the car to pay my respects to the waitress (like in *The Milkman Always Rings Twice*), I decided it prudent—it being broad daylight—to remain for the meantime in the house, away from the eyes of curious neighbors. In any case, there was plenty indoors to keep me out of mischief. So I set about accustoming myself to the sheer physicality of the human world—enrolling myself in a self-taught total-immersion crash course, thereby familiarizing myself with human spatialities, binocular vision, and 3-D per-

spectives. Master the small things first, I told myself, the basics, and who knows, I might go for another spin in the car—to
the mall, for example. The parking lot is convenient and safe.
Even-keeled, barefoot, in a seemingly tailor-fitted two-piece
(African?) gray serge suit and a starched white collar garnished
with a loosened, rakish necktie (from my master's abandoned
wardrobe?) I padded about from one room to the next, confirm-
ing for myself the geography and layout of the residence Hash.

I could now open doors for myself—no need to wait for someone to open them for me. I tried pushing one or two, rocking
them on their hinges to gauge their weight and resistance
should the need ever arise, for example, to flee from some pur-
suant murder investigation along a door-rich hospital base-
ment corridor with the doors getting smaller and smaller (and
the ceiling sloping down at an angle). In a sonorous but pleas-
antly robotic baritone and with an astronaut's precision, I nar-
rated my own actions in the audio-course house-style: *"I am
walking toward the door, I am turning the handle, I am picking
up the book,"* now and then pausing to try my hand at various
wholesome time-saving appliances—such as the valet overnight suit press. Talking of suits, Bob's half of the wardrobe
contained a neatly pressed row of identical, calendrically arranged two-piece pin-striped 24/7 Big Boss business types, one
of which appeared to be missing. It was like being inside an
IKEA catalogue come to life, or a gigantic dollhouse with the
roof off—all very modern in that retro, stuck-in-a late-1950s-
early-1960s-time-warp course-book kind of way. There were
rounded corners on the stove top, there were ducks above the
mantelpiece, and there were those high saloon-style stools at
the breakfast bench in the kitchen. In every single room there
was a three-foot-diameter wall clock. For the first time, I was
able to rifle through Bob's home-study work desk (located for
some reason in the living room) with my own two hands. A
nearby bookcase was occupied by a richly embossed catalogue-
order set of encyclopedias, as yet unconsulted.

Frequently consulted, on the other hand, were duplicate

copies of the Acme Institute course book *Forward with English!*
These I found distributed throughout the house in strategic
locations—popping up like mushrooms on a kitchen counter, on
a proverbial coffee table, on a window ledge in the downstairs
toilet, on the phone table in the hall, too many to mention in all.
Bookmarked in the traditional manner or spread-eagled over
the fat arm of a settee, they each appeared to have been suddenly abandoned at some particular section: Verbs for Special
Occasions, Adjectives for Big Business—as if someone had been
mid-cram for an important certificate exam and had decided to
just walk out of the house and not come back, like the tale of
the *Mary Celeste*. There was even a copy of *Forward with English!* on the bedside commode in the upstairs master bedroom.

And it was at this bedside grammar that I happened to be
browsing (still barefoot and with the insouciant necktie, si-
lently mouthing along to the section on First Steps), where my
flow was interrupted by the *click-tack clack-tick* of a woman's
heels coming along Remington Drive, the velvet rhythm and
impact with which I was only too familiar.

I suspended my reading. Holding my breath and holding my
place (*this is a finger*) with my finger, I threw a look toward the
bedroom window and from my angle of vision observed a pointy
fifties-style ladies' sling-back entering from the left-hand pane.
I caught it just in time to see it scrunch into the pea stone that
bedded the piebald spat-like tires of the Plymouth Fury. The
shoe was strapped snugly to a foot that was attached in turn to
a calf, protruding, with a nice shapely curve from the hem of a
light summer raincoat. I did not need to ascend any higher to
know the foot belonged to Matilda. It was like that bit in *The
Cat in the Hat* where Mother's ankle in the frame of the window
is spied by the goldfish from its startled Cassandrian teapot.

But how much easier to explain the mess in *The Cat in the
Hat* story than to explain the mess in mine!

First Steps!

You find yourself inside the picture book world of an English-language teaching manual for second-language users. From the following list, choose the one that offers the most plausible explanation as to how you might have got there:

a) You are at the theatre for a contemporary production of *Six Cartoon Characters in Search of a Grammarian.* During the intermission you decide to stretch your legs, soon getting lost in the theatre's maze of faded Victorian corridors and brass-banistered Escher-like stairways. At length you come to a dwarf-size door, partly obscured by a red velvet curtain. Having ducked through the little door, you find yourself in the picture book protagonist's garden, vividly replete with flower beds, lawn sprinkler, white picket fence, and apple-pie wife, who appears to be summoning you from the veranda. The little door (marked on the picture book side MISCELLANEOUS PROP

CLOSET) has shut fast behind you with no sign of door-knob or key, or

b) Your town has been dismantled overnight by a fastidious team of malignant demons. Every last building—from the mock colonial bungalows with dormer windows and white picket fences to the bright-fronted chain stores and offices, from the cinema multiscreen and mall complex to the Hotel Bristol—has by morning been replaced by its full-scale life-size LEGOLAND equivalent. Along with the other traumatized inhabitants, you awake to find your command of your own mother tongue, English, is all but gone and henceforth you will be obliged to spend a great portion of your time attending classes in order to learn a replacement processed-cheese dialect in a hermetically sealed reality-TV environment from which there is little chance of escape. The businessman's narrow-brimmed fedora has meanwhile undergone a dramatic revival, or

c) You are Orpheus Hash, erstwhile Argonaut, enchanter of rock and tree, come to rescue from the picture book the slender flower-gathering Eurydice Matilda. On the brink of escorting her away from *Forward with English!* you turn to her claiming to be descended from parrots, whereupon she is snatched once more from your arms. Heartbroken, having blown your chance to be reunited, you then scorn the advances of the Thracian women at the feast of Bacchus, who, perceiving themselves spurned, tear you limb from limb. Your decapitated head and inflatable lyre bob over the sea to the island of Lesbos, where (according to epic tradition) you regale the island inhabitants with exercises (oral) from the grammarian picture book, or

d) Bearing an uncanny resemblance to the lead protagonist in a grammarian picture book (of whose parallel gestalt-switch existence you had hitherto only ever been partially aware), you have been unwittingly commandeered for some kind of set-piece demonstration, apparently now gone horribly wrong, for the Everday Accidents and Domestic Mishaps page, or

e) You are a grammarian detective. It is half past midnight. You have just received by telephone a reliable tip-off that a nonsense virus has managed to hack its way into the course material for *Forward with English!* where under the cloak of anonymity it has already begun to wreak untold havoc. You don raincoat, hat, and gun and set off into the alleys and shadows of the rainy night in pursuit. . . .

An hour or so before my second spectacular metamorphosis, Bob T. Hash III had packed into his maroon-hued, zip-shut traveling suitcase a pair of freshly ironed sky-blue polyester shirts, a fat bestselling detective thriller, and his businessman's toiletry kit (*Br. Eng.: "businessman's sponge bag"*). According to his time-honored agenda, Bob was about to take a short day-away flight to attend an afternoon conference in a neighboring state, and was due to fly back to Belmont that same evening. But the very fact he was taking a plane at all meant he was obliged by picture book protocol to pack the standard business trip luggage (please see page 15 of the picture book, where standard business trip luggage is shown neatly laid out beside the waiting suitcase). Bob put the things inside the suitcase, zipped up the lid, checked his wrist-watch, ticket, and passport, and made his way downstairs. In the hallway he unhooked a light-colored raincoat, folding it over his arm with the briefcase. At the top of the porch steps he pecked his wife good-bye like in an advertisement for cornflakes and climbed into a bright yellow taxi that, as if by magic, had drawn up in front of the house.

"*The Belmont International Airport, my good man!*"

However, the person thereat deposited some twenty minutes later was unrecognizable as the person whom, from the vantage point of my all-seeing window perch, I had watched board the taxi twenty minutes beforehand. This was because, as I would later find out, during his trajectory through leafy grid-pattern suburb and along the new ring route to the airport on the other side of Belmont, Bob had replaced his drab gray necktie with a fluorescent shimmering palm tree clip-on and had slicked a fake tan onto his face. To his scalp he had applied a more generous dollop of Brylcreem than usual and replaced his trademark thick-rimmed Clark Kent spectacles with a pair of wire-rimmed mafia-style Starsky and Hutch sunglasses, affixing to his upper lip a drooping jet-black Zapata false mustache he'd procured from a practical-joke shop—the overall effect being to turn Bob into the spitting image of Señor Gonzalez, principal protagonist and Bob's own counterpart from the Spanish course *¡Vámonos—adelante con el Español!*, whose self-contained picture book universe ran parallel to Bob's own and in many respects shared the same basic format and lifestyle. In any case, anyone who had not watched Bob get into his taxi could have been forgiven for thinking it was Señor Gonzalez, and not Mr. Hash, who got out of the taxi at the airport.

The reason Bob had taken this rather odd step of disguising himself as Señor Gonzalez was that he had decided that he was not going to board his conference-bound flight as per his busy businessman's picture book schedule at all. The original, the irreplaceable Bob T. Hash III, captain of industry, grammarian of the people, favorite citizen of Belmont, today of all days was going to take the unprecedented step of actually *absconding* from the picture book—and he had decided that disguising himself as Señor Gonzalez was the best way to make that escape. From the evidence of two earlier but halfhearted trial escapes (slipping out of a meeting into an unscheduled fire drill; hijacking a battery-powered milk cart that then became entangled with Signor Brambilla's impatient Ferrari—*see also* Accidents Involving Italians), Bob suspected that any attempt to stray any distance in his own guise as Mr. Hash was likely to come up against gentle but firm resistance whereby he, Mr. Bob T. Hash III, would be reined back into the fold. He concluded that extricating himself from the gravitational clutches of the picture book required both greater guile and greater sheer physical speed. He had further observed that, despite the many trumpeted similarities between his own picture book universe and the Spanish one, Señor Gonzalez seemed, generally speaking, to get more leeway than he himself did. Señor Gonzalez was allowed to turn up late for meetings, for example; Señor Gonzalez got to take siestas. Bob noted that on weekends when he himself had to mow the lawn, Señor Gonzalez was allowed to lie in his garden hammock by the lee of an orange tree and smoke a cigar. Señor Gonzalez always seemed to be jetting off to Acapulco on vacation. Hence Señor Gonzalez, hence a flight to Acapulco . . .

On that glorious sunlit morning there would depart from Belmont International Airport a plane bound for Acapulco, its runway takeoff divinely synchronized with the more modest lurch of a certain bird stand back on Remington Drive. For this Bob T. Hash III, alias Señor Gonzalez, possessed in his pocket two valid tickets—one for himself and the other for Miss Scarlett, his personal secretary whose stenographic skills would no doubt prove as indispensable in exile as they had done in the picture book office. Bob had in fact been conducting a clandestine romantic affair with Miss Scarlett for some time and now, putting his romance to good use, he believed that having Miss Scarlett—disguised as Señora Gonzalez—perched on his arm would lend a certain Latinate authenticity to his impersonation of Señor Gonzalez as he passed through the flight gate and thereby increase the likelihood of escape.

Generally speaking, the inhabitants of Belmont are a contented people, and the last thing one might expect is for Bob, as its chief citizen and picture book linchpin, to try to run away from it. ("So, that's two one-way tickets for Acapulco. Cash or credit, sir?") On the other hand, Bob didn't want to risk having any Goody Two-Shoes invisible hand stepping in again to right any wobbles, as per that improvised fire drill (he'd set the alarm off himself using a miniature mallet on the pane of a miniature window in a quiet part of the accounts department's corridor) or

the farcical jaunt on the milk cart. Bob was entering quite un-
charted territory here; nobody had ever tried to abscond from
the *Forward with English!* picture book before—the very idea
seemed absurd! Who could tell what to expect? In many ways
Bob was embarking upon as intrepid and as foolhardy a journey
as those taken by pre-Columbian mariners when they first
made their way toward the curling weir lip at the edge of a flat
earth ocean.

Which is why he'd had to go to all this bother with the disguise. Anyone wondering why he—that is, Bob—wasn't aboard
his scheduled business flight might think he'd taken the initia-
tive to rig up a glitch scenario to be incorporated into a more
nuanced future version of the Departures and Arrivals page—
and so might focus their initial attentions, for example, on how
the meeting might cope without his attendance, as opposed to
tracking down an escapee. While if he, as Bob T. Hash III, was
meanwhile spotted hanging around the airport after his scheduled flight had taken off, Bob knew that an alternative flight
would be arranged on the spur of the moment to make sure
that he made it to his meeting on time. (*No problem, Mr. Hash,
no problem at all. We were just thinking of slotting in an
extra flight when we saw you!*) Sooner or later, of course, his
absence—his real absence—would be noted. But by taking these
precautions Bob hoped that by the time any real alarm bells
started to ring, he and Miss Scarlett would be well beyond any
gravitational pull of *Forward with English!* and so be free at
last from its clutches.

So, when he got out of the taxi, instead of heading to his
usual flight gate, Bob T. Hash III, alias Señor Gonzalez (inhab-
itant of the Spanish colonial villa with an orange tree and hammock in the garden) took himself to the airport mezzanine
cafeteria, from where he could keep an eye on things in the concourse below—a huge vaulted space filled with the echo of heels
and the muted cathedral-like babble of voices, all dwarfed by
the smoke-tinted sheet of plate glass and the space-age sweep
of the architect's roof; all of which contributed to a late 1950s,

early 1960s planes-with-propellers feel to the place. Sheltering behind yesterday's edition of *El País* and the down-turned brim of his fedora, Bob was sipping on a jet-setting milk shake when he heard the seductive spaceship aquarium voice of the woman on the public-address system announcing the details of his flight—that is, the one that Bob T. Hash III was supposed to be going on.

Minutes later, still rooted to his little table, Bob watched passing through his flight gate an ordered gaggle of persons: the marketing men; commission motivation managers; mid-ranking salespeople; qualified hydrologists; nattily dressed grammarians; and the ubiquitous, feisty, nearsighted grand-mother with her equally feisty trolley case—his regular companions in flight. The line (*Br. Eng.: "queue"*) passed through the gate, all boarded the plane, all were now fixing their seat belts and having a quick last flick through the emergency landing procedures—everybody except for the Spanish millionaire with the milk shake.

A last-call announcement brought out a big glistening bead of sweat on the middle of Bob's forehead: this was because Bob knew that this was the last moment there'd be a chance to back-track, to bang down that globe-trotting milk shake, shake off any crazy notion he'd ever had of running away from his picture book life! Still time to rip off that false mustache, dash across the airport concourse, and pant up to the flight gate where Pilot Armstrong would be there to personally tear his ticket stub and the nice-looking hostess would hand him his complimentary gin and tonic: *"Glad you could make it in time, Mr Hash! Here, let me help you with that suitcase."*

But minutes later, having resisted, with palpitating heart and emboldened blue eyes, Bob watched his silver jumbo jet being escorted through the shadow thrown by the building he sat in like a milk cart. Against a backdrop of gray-pink run-ways shimmering in the pallid morning heat he watched the upswooping trails of spent carbon turn mauve-brown through the window's Polaroid filter. The roar of its jet engines was overdubbed by the hissing sound of a short-skirted waitress frothing some milk with the proboscular nozzle of an imported coffee machine. Bob's imagination instinctively ran forward to the scene at lunchtime's seminar: *"Gentlemen, I'm afraid Mr. Hash has missed his flight. Let us hope he can catch the next one and be with us for the afternoon session. Let us proceed in the meantime with a preview of last quarter's sales figures. . . ."*

That Bob's scheduled conference-bound plane was able to leave the runway tarmac at all without his being actually aboard it was the first concrete evidence that his own destiny was not so utterly welded to that of the picture book that Belmont could not survive without its lead protagonist at least for a few moments—and who knows for how much longer. Encouraged by this knowledge, Bob checked his wristwatch, made a minute straightening adjustment to his mustache, and deposited a generous pile of pesetas by the polystyrene container of his two-thirds empty milk shake. It was time for his rendezvous with Miss Scarlett.

Miss Scarlett was waiting for him, as per their arrangement, at the international news kiosk, browsing through the Spanish edition of *Good Housekeeping* disguised in film-starlet's sunglasses, a three-day solarium tan, and a glamorous silk "anchors-and-knots" head scarf. With studied casualness and no word of greeting, Bob settled his suitcase farther along at the car magazines and began, at random, *broom-broom,* to read one; both browsing, like strangers at a bookshop, oblivious of each other's existence. Not till an announcement came over the PA system did they look up from their magazines and exchange a stolen look of acknowledgment through their respective pairs of inscrutable sunglasses.

It was the announcement telling passengers intending to take the flight for Acapulco to assemble at gate 17.

4

Asking for Directions—
"nel mezzo del cammino"

You are Señor Gonzalez, attending an important business conference being held at an idyllic Alpine resort. On a free afternoon you go for a stroll along the lakeside promenade. Returning from your walk, you discover your hotel has gone missing. The site where the hotel once stood seems to now be carpeted with a variety of dried nuts and seeds.

(Note to language instructor: Student is to imagine approaching various passersby for help. In each of the following skits, the passerby will give one of five possible responses. Student is to select the response that, in his opinion, would most likely put him back on track. In this exercise students may be blindfolded and "twirled round" to enhance a feeling of genuine disorientation.)

a) The first person you decide to ask is a tall man in a pin-striped dinner suit, with a bow tie and Brylcreemed hair. He has just crossed the road with a fawning gait and has a silver tray tucked under his arm. Why not ask him?

You: Excuse me, sir, could you tell me where the Hotel Bristol is?

Man in a Dinner Suit:

(i)   I'm afraid the lamb is off today, sir.

(ii) No, I think you'll find that our other customers actually quite appreciate the air-conditioning and would prefer me to keep it switched on.

(iii) It's delivered from the industrial kitchens by the quickest means on the market.

(iv) No, I said you cannot use the back of my tray as a mirror.

(v)   Just fill out a complaint form and leave it in the box and I'll make sure the duty manager sees it.

b) That was bad luck. But look, there at the side entrance to that very grand edifice with mansard roofs and a row of flags over the portico, there's a man in white flannels and a tall pastry chef's hat taking a cigarette break. Perhaps he'll be more helpful?

You: Excuse me, sir, but I'm not terribly familiar with the street plan around here. You couldn't perhaps direct me to the Hotel Bristol?

White-Hatted Chef:

(i)   No, thanks, I don't smoke.

(ii) Leave in low oven for an hour and forty minutes, basting now and again.

(iii) No, this hotel does not lend out maps.

(iv) Now knead gently—adding yeast.

(v)   Je suis velly solly, I no speako English today please.

c) Sitting on a lakeside bench admiring snow-topped mountains is the chambermaid who changed your bed linen

this morning. Could she perhaps apprise you of your
mislaid hotel's whereabouts?

> You: I hate to disturb you, but I wonder if you could
> direct me to the Hotel Bristol.

> CHAMBERMAID WITH DOILY APRON, FEATHER DUSTER,
> LONG BLACK LASHES:
> (i)   No, sir, we only change them once a day.
> (ii)   I'll be bringing more complimentary soaps
>   tomorrow.
> (iii)   Take it by the corners and we can fold it
>   together.
> (iv)   It was destroyed by fire a few years back.
> (v)   Right enough, sir, it's corked: I'll just nip down
>   to our cellar to fetch another bottle.

d) The olive-skinned almond-eyed trilingual receptionist
with the jet-black ponytail from the Hotel Bristol is
reading a book and sipping an espresso under an umbrella at that lakeside café at the end of her shift. Maybe
you'll have more luck with her?

> You: Good afternoon, Miss, I would be most obliged if
> you could show me the way to the Hotel Bristol.

> OLIVE-SKINNED ALMOND-EYED TRILINGUAL RECEPTION-
> IST WITH JET-BLACK PONYTAIL FROM THE HOTEL BRIS-
> TOL AT THE END OF HER SHIFT:
> (i)   It's not bad so far, but I'm not quite sure where
>   it's all leading to.
> (ii)   Yes, "al dente omelette"—you're right, it
>   doesn't make sense. I'll pass that on to the lady
>   who writes out our menus.
> (iii)   It would spoil the ending if I told you!
> (iv)   I believe it's in Bristol.
> (v)   Well, okay—but remember I have to be back
>   for the start of my next shift.

e) Nobody seems to have been very helpful so far. Now try that little news kiosk selling postcards and maps run by the gentleman with the cloth cap (bearing a striking resemblance to Bert from the kiosk in Belmont).

> You (surprised): Ah, Bert, so it *is* you! And what might bring you to this neck of the woods?
>
> Indefatigable Ubiquitous Loyal Factotum Bert Peering Askance at Your False Mustache: Good to see you again, Mr. Hash. Let's just say I'm filling in here as a holiday favor. How may I be of service today?
>
> You Again: Well, actually, Bert (scraping seed from shoes), I was wondering if someone could tell me how to get to the Hotel Bristol.
>
> Indefatigable Ubiquitous Loyal Indigenous-Cartographer Bert, Unfolding Street Plan from His Stall: Certainly, Mr. Hash. . . . Now, let me see. Well (pointing along the lakefront), see that big building over there, that's the back of the mall. Your office building is only a few yards away from the entrance . . . but you'll know your way from there, I guess, Mr. Hash!
>
> You, Suddenly No Longer Concerned About Ever Finding the Hotel Bristol: Sure will, Bert—and thanks once again for your help. Let's just run through that again to make sure I got it. . . .

5

The moment I recognized Matilda's sleek feline calf in the bedroom window against the pea-stone drive—my heart most strangely a-patter—I dashed into the en suite bathroom to straighten my necktie. Quite who I thought I was going to pass myself off for, and quite how I was going to explain how that person, whoever they might be, had come to be in her house, I hadn't worked out yet. But, according to some absurd logic forged on the spur of the moment, I decided that if I could at least do up my top shirt buttons and amend my blindly constructed Windsor, then Matilda might find the idea of an intruder a little less surprising—or more to the point, a little less disagreeable. Perhaps then she would be more willing to give the benefit of the doubt—who better to explain such a bizarre story than a well-dressed business gentleman with a genuine Windsor?

Yet what a surprise I myself got when I reached the bathroom sink and took hold of the flailing strands of my weightless experimental necktie. So perfect was the resemblance, so uncanny the likeness, that for several moments I actually thought I was looking not at my reflection in a mirror but through a window at Bob T. Hash III, who, for reasons of his own, had decided to backtrack from the airport after all. Had he himself dashed into the adjacent room with the same bright idea of straightening his necktie? At some newly constructed window between here and some freshly constructed bathroom.

There was the same swept-back mane of Brylcreemed hair, that same manly mandible jawline, the same air of affable tycoon, like a youthfully middle-aged Robert Lowell who, laying aside a tortured poem on the weekend and throwing off his cardigan, might play Frisbee on the lawn with his children.

I stuck out my arms like a windmill, and Bob did a windmill arm back. I put a thumb to my nose and waggled my fingers like a one-armed air flautist, and Bob did this too. I tried on the spare pair of Bob's thick-rimmed Clark Kent glasses (perched by the toothbrush container on the ledge of the sink) and saw that the same quizzical not-got-a-clue-what's-going-on-here-Miss-Lane look that Bob sometimes has on his face was now on the face I could now call my own.

Considering the potentially infinite permutations of physiognomic features I might have actually found myself with in my human disguise, it seemed an uncanny stroke of luck that I turned out to have been cloned from Bob T. Hash III. On the other hand, on a little reflection, such duplication may not be quite as far-fetched as you might think. Though I'd be hard-pushed to explain the actual molecular workings behind my pharmacologically inspired metamorphosis, one can well imagine that whatever principles governed the grosser physical change, they may well be related, at the cellular level, in an analogous way, to my natural gift for mimicry. The logic being that if my parrot self was ever going to adopt human form, it would most naturally take the form of the person who had taught it the rudiments of civilized speech.

My tie as straight as a plumb line, I ran out of the en suite bathroom and bounded down the stairs. By the time Matilda's latchkey scraped in the front door lock, I was back in the living room. The poor cage was dead. Surveying the mess, I realized with sudden full force the patent absurdity of my situation: What was a duplicate of her husband up to in her living room, and where on earth was the mascot household parrot when we needed him? I was simply going to have to bite the bullet and ride along with the clone business—pretending I really *was* Mr.

Hash. I was going to have to explain three distinct things to his wife: 1) the fallen bird stand and chaos of seed; 2) one missing African gray parrot; 3) why her husband (not due back from his business trip till the evening) was back so soon. Somehow I was going to have to tie these things up into one plausible, compact little story—and get it right the first time.

It was a gamble, but I had an idea. While Matilda was still in the hallway, there was just enough time to open a living room window. After a moment, when she came into the room in her nice unbuttoned beige raincoat, she found me arms akimbo, pacing to and fro over the mess, shaking my head from side to side in quiet businessman's disbelief. It was as if I had not long ago arrived on the scene myself and was still trying my hardest to digest it—which was anyway not so far off the truth.

Matilda threw off the rest of her redundant summer raincoat and raised her hands to her mouth.

"I can't see what kind of grammatical construction they're getting at here at all," I said—in an authentic Bob T. Hash III voice—"unless it has something to do with an Everday Accidents and Domestic Mishaps page for the forthcoming edition of *Forward with English!*" *Bob T. Hash III had missed his plane and decided to take the day off.*

But Matilda was more concerned with the whereabouts of her parrot—precious, beloved—than any apparent hiccup in her busy husband's travel schedule.

"Comenius."

She half sobbed, poignantly kneeling down to pick up the little ladder with her long slender fingers.

"Yes. Poor Comenius must have taken fright and flown out the window."

But look on the bright side, I might well have added—*he didn't fall five floors to his death on bone-smashing flagstones.*

"He's probably just perching on a neighbor's white picket fence."

And, of course, I *did* feel a bit bad that my first words to Matilda, now in the role of my wife, had to be a fiction in this

way, and a painful fiction at that, given the great fondness she
had always reserved for her parrot. But I was also aware how
unbelievable, how fantastic, any even approximately truthful
account would have come across. On the other hand I think
you'll agree that, morally speaking, my little white lie pales into
insignificance if you compare it to the stories her husband had
been telling her of late, vis-à-vis his so-called "extra workload"
at the office.

Now, remember, I had at this point no idea how long I would
remain, and with what degree of stability, under the guise of
the good Bob T. Hash III. However, I did possess one useful
piece of inside information that gave me at least some peace of
mind. From a series of whispered phone conversations, made
within earshot of my perch, on a number of evenings leading up
to my mentor's departure, I was privy to the fact of Bob's secret
elopement with Miss Scarlett. Outside the parties involved, I
alone knew that Bob was away on far more than a simple routine business trip, I alone knew he had no intention of returning either to his wife or to his picture book duties. In other
words, so long as nobody got cold feet or the elopement had been
otherwise thwarted, my taking over as Mr. Hash for a little
while was unlikely to be challenged—from those quarters at
least.

In any case, I wouldn't have been surprised if by dinner-
time, say, the effects of the cuttlebone had faded, with me returned as parrot to my perch as after my spin under the stars.
At which point the only thing left to resolve would be the mysterious non-return of Bob T. Hash III from his business trip—
but that would be his problem, not Comenius's. And even if the
cuttlebone's magical effects should last into the night and Bob,
having got cold feet, decided to turn up at midnight with his tail
between his legs—well, even then the worst thing that could
really happen would be my having to act out some bedroom
farce situation in which a twin Bob is seen hiding in the
wardrobe.

As it turned out, the rest of that eventful day passed off

without further disaster. Playing at being Bob T. Hash III was really rather easy—a harmless if somewhat audacious pastime. Matilda and I went round each room of the house in turn, searching for Comenius, checking that he (which is to say, I) hadn't flown into some shaded recess of the house rather than out through the window, as suggested. Having in vain conducted that search, we returned to the living room to reassemble the scattered elements of the bird stand and to clean up the mess (a bit like that big cleaning contraption in *The Cat in the Hat*—all waggling sprocket, gangling fop-brush, and articulate dustpan). We righted the fallen elm branch wedged vertically in its bucket of ballast cement, reattached the birdcage to its bough, reaffixed the appurtenances (mercifully, nothing was broken). Birdseed and downy gray feathers were vacuumed off the carpet, and a light spattering of guano was daubed off the hearth tiles with a warm soapy sponge.

Amazingly, at no point during these operations did either my wife or the children (with whom I played a game of post-homework, pre-dinner indoor Frisbee) show suspicion of foul play. At one point as we were nearing the end of the cleanup operation, Matilda did ask, "Nothing to do in the office?" with an eyebrow raised, having perhaps detected a chink in the logic of my impersonation—would the original Bob have ever claimed there was *nothing to do* in the office? But rather than get angry and say, *"My husband would never say a thing like there's nothing to do in the office—you dastardly impostor,"* Matilda just smiled like a regular Lady Macbeth and went on, "Well, you might have gone in and done a few of those *'Is this a book,' 'Is that a pencil,'* to keep your hand in."

But that enigmatic little exchange apart, nobody seemed to twig that this well-dressed six-foot parrot was neither their father nor their husband, or that Comenius was among them even as they searched for him, like the apostles searching for Jesus. *That's right, Tom, there's been a downturn in sales.*

So confident of my impersonation had I become that later, as Matilda was clearing away the dinner dishes, I felt bold enough to plant a moist peck on her cheek. She was bending over the table to retrieve a tureen from its mat of asbestos, wearing an apron with wipe-proof grammatical tips and an easy one-tug bow-knot. I looped a wild strand of hair behind her ear. It would have been difficult to loop by herself with her hands full.

At which point certain further potential ramifications of my replicant status first dawned in my mind.

At any event, for that night at least, my condition remained stable. I did not turn back into a parrot. Bob did not cop out of his elopement. To the best of my knowledge there were no sitcom farces from daytime TV involving clanging hangers in hollow wooden wardrobes.

6

Introductions: How Do You Do?

In everyday life we sometimes run over people we've not met before (*see* Idiomatic Expressions) or people whom we've only heard of through hearsay. For this section, the teacher can refer to the illustration on page 14 of the picture book showing Client-Speak for Intermediate Level conference attendees taking advantage of a moment's break in the convention foyer to make one another's acquaintance.

(Note to teacher: For skit enactments please cover name tags!)

— Mr. Cash, this is Mr. Redford. Mr. Redford, this is Mr. Cash. Mr. Redford, this is Mr. Bickwick. Mr. Bickwick, this is Mr. Redford. Mr. Redford, this is Mr. Hash . . . Mr. Hash? . . . Oops, Mr. Hash seems to have slipped off somewhere—I expect he'll be back to join us in a moment!

(later, at the cocktail party)
— . . . and this will be your good lady wife, Mr. Hash?

— As a matter of fact, this is my secretary, Miss Scarlett. I've an important deadline to get something ready for next week's announcement of the quarterly sales figures and I've brought her along to the conference to help me out with her stenographic skills.

(*still at the cocktail party!*)

BOB T. HASH III: I'd like you to meet my better half, Mrs. Hash.

CUCKOLDING NARRATOR, PECKING THE BACK OF A SLENDER OUTSTRETCHED WRIST: The pleasure is mine . . .

(*next morning, back in the convention foyer*)

JACK: Mr. Hash, I'd like to introduce you to my colleague Bob T. Hash III.

MR. HASH: Good to meet you, Bob. How do you do? We do seem to keep crossing each other's paths, so it's good at last to meet you in person.

BOB T. HASH III: I've been looking forward to meeting you too, Bob. Jack tells me you're destined for great things!

MR. HASH: Well, let's put it this way: I won't be jumping out any fifth-floor office windows for the foreseeable future!

The twin Bobs exchange business cards and shake hands.

7

Matutinal routines are the backbone of civilization. They begin, innocently enough, with the song of a melodious window-ledge blue tit and the hum of an electric milk cart. In the ablutive phase alone, they compress sufficient reflexive verbs—to bathe, shave, brush, floss, and so forth—to last most of us the rest of the day. On an easy-wipe blue-checked tablecloth appears an ideal home demonstration breakfast—replete with a variety of hen-eggs (poached, boiled, scrambled, and fried), breakfast cereals, and gelatinous preparations of the citrus persuasion. In the office a day of busy appointments awaits our arrival.

For the first few moments that next morning when I was woken up by Bob T. Hash III's digital alarm clock, I actually thought I was Comenius the parrot, back on my perch; I couldn't understand why the electric buzz of the alarm, also audible from the downstairs living room bird stand, was so near to my ear and so annoyingly loud. I hit the snooze button the way Bob does in the seventh edition of the picture book and lay there for a minute or two listening to sounds coming from the kitchen, which, as the fog of sleep began to lift, I recognized as the sounds of Matilda getting the children ready to go off to school and preparing Bob's breakfast. Only then, stretching out an arm to trace the warm proverbial imprint of Bob's wife on the mattress beside me, did the remarkable events of yesterday—and the even more remarkable events of last night—begin to come back into focus.

Those ablutions, that breakfast, those business appointments stretching on into Bob's day, would now sadly go empty and turn into no-shows. Meetings canceled, deadlines overshot. The whole grammar book world revolving around him—and Bob not even bothering to put in an appearance! On the other hand, my own agenda was empty. Comenius had no prior appointments, had nowhere to be at a quarter to nine in the morning. Comenius did not even possess an agenda. Comenius was as free as a bird and, besides, could turn in a more than passable Bob T. Hash III. What if Comenius put on Bob's suit and tie, ate Bob's breakfast, and went into the office instead? By the time the snooze buzzer came back on I'd made up my mind. For a second time in the space of twenty-four hours I found myself heading barefoot to the Hashes' upstairs en suite bathroom.

One round picture book hour later, Bob T. Hash III's Plymouth Fury gently reversed out the pea-stone drive, the driver bearing a quite uncanny resemblance to the legitimate license holder of that car—a Thunderbird captain with a swashbuckling profile. Viewed through a boom-mounted camera lens craning elastically out from the Hashes' front porch we see a neighbor's dog getting splashed by a sprinkler as it barks at the postman, the camera then curtsying upward for the obligatory panning shot over dormer rooftops and the luminous lawns of Day-Glo Suburbia. And look! Appearing from under the lintel of the Hashes' porch roof a woman's wistful hand was waving the Plymouth Fury good-bye.

If the Hash residence had been a set off of *Bewitched,* then Bob T.'s office in the worldwide headquarters of the Acme International Institute of Languages located on picture book Main Street was *Hill Street Blues* on chamomile tea. It was a bright diorama of Play-Doh pie charts and Tetra Pak filing cabinets; an open-plan arrangement of desk, swivel chair, computer monitor, and ergonomic partition. On my arrival, any fears I might be mistaken for a parrot impostor were quickly dispelled. Bob Hash's trademark briefcase under my arm, I was familiar to all, and all, from my intimate knowledge of *Forward with English!* (editions one through seven), were familiar to me. There was Bert to start off with, at the foyer reception desk downstairs (*"Morning, Mr. Hash. No need to sign the register this morning, sir!"*). I then shared my ascent in the right-hand capsule of the twin-box elevator with Miss Slowcomb, for whom, arriving out of breath, I held open the lift doors with a gallant elbow that brought a blush to her cheek (*"That's right, Mr. Hash. I'm in Admin these days"*). Passing through the abacus to-ings and fro-ings of the top-floor open-plan section to reach my own executive office, I met Janet lugging a box of grammar files (*"Morning, Mr. Hash. No, thanks, I can manage"*). There was Larry Bickwick rummaging in a metal cabinet for an ink cartridge for the photocopier (*"Goodness to Betsy—somebody's been using the photocopier again!"*); there was Chester Cash too, answering an important business phone call (*"Be with you in a sec, Bob!"*). There was Miss Ratcliffe from the human resources department breaking off from issuing an instruction (*"How did your business trip go, Mr. Hash? Oh, there's something I need to speak to you about, by the way"*).

Bob T. Hash's executive office itself, at the end of this marshmallow minefield, had a nameplate on the door that said MR. BOB T. HASH III in big bold letters under the venetian blinds, and anyone who wanted to go through that door and who wasn't Bob T. Hash III in person had to knock first and wait outside for Bob T. Hash's permission to enter. For a moment, I stood there. I didn't knock, but I didn't go in either. This was my Rubicon moment. Either I was Bob T. Hash III and did not need to knock, or I was not Bob T. Hash III and did need to. Funnily enough, despite my inside knowledge regarding Bob's elopement, and even after the welcomes I had just received from his colleagues—I still half expected to look through the venetian blinds and see Bob at his desk with his nose in last month's sales figures.

I looked through the slats. My fears were unfounded. I went through the door without knocking. There was a nice, thick wall-to-wall off-gray carpet and an impressive air-conditioned plushness. Like picture book Bob T. Hash III, I hung my trilby on a prong of the hat stand and, before sitting down, went over to get a quick look out the window—down down down to the quiet well-tended toy-town, a dizzying five stories below. Along Main Street cars were floating by as meek as electrical milk carts, and pedestrians were sliding along sidewalks as if on casters. The sidewalks were so tidy and clean they might have been scrubbed down only that morning. At Peccary's department store opposite, I watched a truck delivering haberdashery supplies—a fine bolt of cloth, a bumper consignment of trilbies stacked in cartons. In its window display a mannequin in a Lacoste polo shirt and sun visor was readying to putt for a birdie.

I came away from the window, did a lap of the desk, and sat down in Bob's comfy executive chair. Leaning back, cupping my hands at the back of my head, I surveyed diverse objects arranged on the pale burgundy leather canvas of the desk top—an oversize black Bakelite telephone with an old-fashioned ring dial and externally mounted bells; a framed photo of the Hash family posed in front of the house porch on Remington Drive; a mercury-filled executive stress toy with a little ladder (that I was later to break); and, oh yes, in the out-tray section of an otherwise empty three-tiered plastic stack arrangement there was a large manila envelope that jumped out at me as looking strangely familiar.

The three-bunk-tiered office work tray can be made of either plastic or aluminum; while manilas—the whole-wheat mulatto of the envelope world—exude by design a dull bluff anonymity that is off-putting enough for an addressee, let alone an impartial, truth-seeking bystander such as myself. When plastic, as in the case of Bob T. Hash III's, the tray arrangement (in, out, pending) alas didn't display the same range of color that my rungs did. All the more surprising then that my interest should

have been piqued, all the more unexpected that the manila envelope should—I nearly said *in a jiffy*—find itself in my hands.

"Could this envelope contain the manuscript that Bob had
been so busy with in the run-up to his dramatic elopement?" I
reached over and palpated the dense sheaf of paper inside
the manila. It's true, Bob had been bringing more work home of
late than usual—to work on at his living room desk in the
evenings—as if he'd been working on some extracurricular
project, with its own stringent deadline; and it's true he did
keep his work in a manila envelope, just like the one I was now
holding in my hands.

What valiant ping-pong monograph had so obsessed Bob,
what learned thesis had taken up so many of his final reflective
evenings? Perhaps some tractatus on marketing strategy, an
omnibus of business terms, or some glossy brochure on phrasal
verbs? Well, if I was right about the manila, then I was perhaps
about to find out. As I undid the envelope's metal wing clips I
had a strange foreboding that I was about to unveil some important further clue in connection to Bob's disappearance—that
I was on the brink of discovering some significant riddle-like
link between my mentor's unscheduled departure and my own
even bolder misadventure.

I had barely time to browse through a page or so of Asking
for Directions when there was a knock on my executive door imperious enough to rattle the venetians. It was Miss Ratcliffe
from Human Resources. When Miss Ratcliffe entered the office
and bid Bob once again a good morning, my first inclination was
to fly up onto a spare prong of the hat stand and go *"Morning,
Mr. Hash! . . . Morning, Mr. Hash!* in the classic, screechy
singsong who's-a-pretty-Polly parrot voice, for which parrots
are indeed rightly famed. Fortunately for the hat stand, and my
budding career as a Bob T. Hash III, I desisted, for Miss Ratcliffe was dropping by, on a personal basis, to bring me bad
news. In her own courtesy call voice (that I recognized from
Acme Business Audiocassette 3), Miss Ratcliffe informed me
that Miss Scarlett, my personal assistant, had not come into

the office today. Since it was most unusual for Miss Scarlett to turn up late for work, the department of human resources was naturally anxious that something untoward might have happened. "We've tried calling her at her home, but no one's answering the phone."

This was a grave loss indeed on my first day at work! To show my concern, I put on the same expression of disappointment I'd seen one day on Bob's face, when his lawn mower had run out of gas. I laid down the manuscript though not letting it entirely out of my grasp in the off chance someone (not necessarily Miss Ratcliffe) might make a lunge across the desk for it and dash out of the office. Miss Ratcliffe said she knew how important and busy I was and so had brought me a temporary replacement—a timorous stenographer who up to this point in the conversation had been hiding behind Miss Ratcliffe and who was now introduced to me as Miss Happ. In the event that the matter remained unresolved, Miss Ratcliffe's efficient team was as we spoke already vetting a new batch of applicants for a permanent replacement. I expressed both my thanks for Miss Ratcliffe's sensitive, efficient handling of the matter and my concern regarding the well-being and whereabouts of Miss Scarlett. I said that if there were any developments she should let me know at once.

"Don't worry, Mr. Hash," she said. "If we get any news, you'll be the first person to know."

She'd said "person." I looked up at the oversize wall clock three feet across in the face: it was just gone a quarter past nine.

8

Asking For and Telling the Time
—It's half past a quarter to twelve

Note to the language instructor: Open teacher's picture manual at the clock page (page 9) and prop up against a vertical surface in front of class. Students will readily identify the in-house artist's impression of various iconic timepieces depicted with terpsichorean flair—the Viennese waltzing mantelpiece baroque; a noble pin-striped Big Ben dancing the Charleston; a Jacques Cousteau deep-sea diver's "Monde-du-Silence" Bangkok Rolex doing the polka; a regal long-cased grandfather clock with Roman numerals doing the military pendulum two-step; a tap-dancing "Matilda Hash–ian" luminous ivory cuckoo with a tiny pink tongue; a living room carriage with classic "dead-beat" escapement mechanism doing the cancan; the somber, charcoal-faced entrance clock over the mad Valletta Arch at Broadmoor; the puppet-ringed astrological clock in Prague's Old Town Square; a doctor's pulse-quickening fob watch; not to mention Mr. Hash's very own digital radio alarm, which woke us up with a businessman's tango on page 38.

Each clock has a different time on it; teacher will point at faces in random order and drill exhaustively with class. Teacher should also make use of other pages of the picture manual where clocks nestle in corner frames of vignetted sequences orchestrating various characters' routines: Miss Scarlett arrives at the office at 8:15; Tushi Moto has lunch at 12:45; at half past eight in the morning Mr. Hash packs his suitcase for a routine business trip, etc.

A blackboard, felt-strip duster, and stick of traditional chalk—preferably a chronographer's white—(not to mention teacher's versatile windmilling forelimbs) may also be useful for this exercise.

Skit

You are on your way to an important business meeting in London. Your wristwatch seems to have stopped and you are worried you might be running late. Big Ben is nowhere to be seen, and there do not appear to be any horologists present. Why not check with that traditional beefeater standing at the corner?

YOU: "Excuse me, Constable. I'm on my way to an important business meeting. My watch seems to have stopped and I'm worried I might be running late. You wouldn't be able to tell me the correct time, please?"

TRADITIONAL BEEFEATER: (pulling watch chain from breast—the big hand is pointing to seven, the little one to three): "Certainly, sir. It's five past nine, sir."

YOU: "Golly, Constable. If I get my skates on, I might just make that meeting after all!"

9

Having dispatched her news regarding the nonappearance of the normally punctual Miss Scarlett (alarm clock malfunction? trapped in a freak traffic jam? kidnapped by alien space invaders?) and no doubt under the indelible impression that she had imparted her tidings to Bob T. Hash III, Miss Ratcliffe returned to her lair in the department of human resources, leaving me to my own devices at the helm of the worldwide organizational headquarters of the Acme International Institute of Languages—publisher of, among other things, the celebrated *Forward with English!*

It's perhaps worth pointing out that Bob T. Hash III is by no means the first paterfamilias and principal protagonist in the course book tradition to find himself in the position of being replaced. In fact, there had been no fewer than six other principal actors before him, each the linchpin to his own edition, each of whom in his time had undergone such a fate. Bob himself had taken over the reins from straw-haired Stan Waldman of stolid reputation from the sixth edition of *Forward with English!* And Stan Waldman had in turn taken over from suave corn exporter Warren Crosby from the fifth. Warren had stepped into the shoes of dapper Hank Redford from the much loved and, at the time, seemingly eternal fourth. Before whom came the avuncular Mr. Cotton from the not-so-long-lived third (atrocious proofreading). Before Mr. Cotton, there was Mr. Phillips, the cigar-smoking garden sprinkler magnate.

And before them all came the inimitable Winfield Norton: pathfinder, prophet, and original template. Though mostly retired and gone from sight, these once exemplary giants of grammatical rectitude do still sometimes bob up (*see* Idiomatic Expressions) for a cameo appearance in later editions—you'll see them turn up for some meeting to bring up the numbers or swan in for the odd round of golf. Mr. Cotton, for example, no longer in the fray of things, has, like a well-meaning President Carter, been recycled as a congenial fellow diner in the coffee shop, and in that new role has proved a far more popular figure than he'd ever been as main protagonist.

What *is* unusual, in Bob's case, is the unorthodox manner of his replacement—not to mention the spectacular fact that his having been replaced at all seems to have escaped everyone's notice. Without exception, and with good grace, Bob's forerunners were replaced, each in turn, according to the tradition whereby they would resign when the edition over which they presided was superseded by a new one, like honorable sea captains going down with their sinking ships. The colors in the old *Forward with English!* come to look sun-bleached and pallid, the décor and props become dog-eared, the exercises grow a tad shabby, the cast a tad jaded. That's when it's time for the stories to get re-plotted, the routines refreshed, the exercises rehashed—with a nod or two to modernity thrown in for good measure (like those funky computer monitors that appeared on the office desks in the sixth edition). That's when it's time for the old edition to be phased out, withdrawn from service and a new, spruced-up version with a client-friendly spill-proof cover to hit the front display counters in the institute foyer. A brand-new protagonist now emerges, providing not only a figure with whom the aspiring linguist will come once again to readily identify, but whose workaday triumphs will again form the loose-fitting plot around which the grammar examples find a natural focus.

In my mind I'd sometimes imagined those deposed grandees gracing now a range of banknotes of varying denominations, now as profiles chiseled democratically into a rock face like the implacable presidents at Mount Rushmore (*Forward with English!* editions one through seven). At other times I'd imagined them as an inspection parade of Russian dolls, with a new one right after Bob—the eighth—a big cartoon question mark hovering over its blank silhouetted face as if some unidentified criminal or a mystery guest on a TV game show. I'd envisioned them as the solemn enigmatic statues of Easter Island staring into the mothballed distance. But as I come to learn no one before Bob actually chose of their own free will to *abandon* his cushy tenure (*see* Active vs. Passive). Bob was the first one to duck out, the first to go AWOL. He is also the first protagonist to have been replaced by a metamorphosed parrot.

I was wondering what might have become of my illustrious antecedents when, Miss Ratcliffe now gone, I read on into the manuscript from where I'd left off. I was impressed, as I'd been before Miss Ratcliffe's interruption, by the presentation, and by a clear sense of purpose. The details—granted the cocoon of its mild late-fifties-early-sixties time warp—were accurate: the picture book picket fence was freshly painted, the lawns evenly irrigated and luminously green, recognizably from our very own dear Belmont.

On the other hand, for all its veneer of professionalism, I was beginning to get the feeling that something faintly peculiar was going on. Clearly, the collection of exercises and pictures I'd found was meant to be some kind of guidebook or grammar primer—not entirely surprising, I suppose, given this was the Acme International Institute of Languages. My hunch was that my discovery had something to do with course material for the new—that is, an eighth—edition of the grammar. After all, the seventh edition had been around now for quite a while (as had Bob) and rumors had been circulating around Belmont for some time now that a new one was in the pipeline. What was surprising, however, was that something about the *content* of the exercises did not quite ring true. Even on my first brief pre–Miss Ratcliffe perusal of the Asking for Directions section, I'd sensed the odd snag, sensed something jarring to my eye, and those same sorts of snags seemed now to be creeping into the section on telling the time—as if the author was somehow winding us up. Don't get me wrong—the overall impression was still convincing; the regular grammar book format and canonical phrase book conventions were adhered to throughout; the layout beyond reproach: I too would have wanted to learn my English from it! Yet something I couldn't quite put my finger on was amiss—more a crypticness of tone, a slight free-flowing freestyle topsy-turvy discombobulation, as it were, than, say, straightforward grammatical or spelling mistakes (though for all I know there may well have been some of those in there too). I put down the manuscript and took off my Clark Kent specs. For the second time that morning I found myself rubbing my chin.

This was turning out to be a strange affair indeed. My own dramatic metamorphosis, the business of Bob's elopement, and the Rubiconic office door with the Bakelite telephone on the office desk. But it was the mystery manuscript, and, more to the point, its riddled idiosyncrasies, that I found strangest of all. What had I stumbled upon, by this somewhat unusual and circuitous route? What might it all add up to? Could this really be the new eighth edition of *Forward with English!*? And, if so, to what degree was Bob involved in its compilation? Might not the oddities simply be some kind of teething problems confined to its opening sections, or some as yet remaining and uncorrected errata-in-progress—which Bob, as editor in chief, had been working on right up till he eloped to Acapulco?

Let's just hope that whatever the cause of the problem it will be rectified in the sections to come.

10

Vocabulary for Beginners

Everyday household objects, instantly recognizable and universally beloved personages, artifacts from Mother Nature—detach themselves from their more familiar contexts with prelapsarian panache. Unmoored, free-floating, and apparently self-propelled, the pulsating nomadic monads take it in turn to approach the student with their mute but cheerful introductions.

To make this exercise more realistic, the world has been blotted out and replaced by a vast amniotic depth of uniform air-conditioned blackness, from which the approaching well-behaved, water-birthed objects emerge. From the blackest void, objects whoosh up toward us on slow-motion comet-shaped orbits, and magnify themselves, urging us like Adam to call them by name. When identified correctly by the student, the object seems to blush, hovering for a modest curtsy that will help imprint the name indelibly on the student's mind, and proceeds on its course. If, on the other hand, the student calls an incorrect name, the object will hold back, egging us on to try again, the mind on the tip of its tongue. If student continues to err, the object must give up and it too (a trifle offended) must pass on, merging back into the starless heavens whence it came, perhaps never to return. In this exercise the student's task is to offer a commentary on the procession. Please note that the indefinite article is preferred:

"Here comes a book; this is a book, and this is a map of the world. Here's Mr. Hash; here comes a hat; here comes a suitcase. Here comes a taxi; here comes a plane; the driver is waving. Here is Matilda; here comes the sky. Here comes some seed; please shut the window; let's have a look in the mirror. Here is a box of cigars; here comes a tree; a spade is a spade. Here comes a house; here comes a sprinkler. This is a clock; here comes a lamp; that rings a bell. This color's turquoise; this is magenta; all swans are white. Here comes a flag; here comes a menu. That man's a fireman; the woman's a nurse; that's a policeman. Here comes a pencil, here comes a rope, here comes a wrench, here comes a mishap. Ecstasy, rapture, a thousand enchantments. Here come the martians; here comes a ladder . . .

. . . and there goes the bell; class dismissed!"

11

From the reaction that his PA's failure to turn up at the office
had caused, one can imagine the even greater distress the news
of Bob's own disappearance would have created—and the ripple
of panic that would have spread among his colleagues as the
true scandal of his elopement came to light. And yet, over the
coming days, no one was to express even the faintest suspicion
that anything was amiss regarding the personal identity of heroically stalwart Bob T. Hash III. Thanks
to my immaculate physical clone likeness and to my
long-suffering observations from various strategically placed
perches; thanks to my familiarity with the picture book epi-
routines; thanks to my considerable natural powers of emu-
lation (voice modulation, mannerisms, gestures, inflection of
mood); and thanks not least to my parrot's mastery of lite-
speak, slotting into my new role of Bob Hash was as easy as—
well, as easy as falling off a log. My intimate knowledge of the
picture book geography and its dramatis personae conferred on
me, besides, a sort of immunity to surprise. From Bert, who
sold me my newspaper at the newsstand in the morning (*"How
much are the* Belmont Gazettes, *please?" "Here's your change,
Mr. Hash. Have a nice day!"*) to hardworking colleagues (*"I'll
have that report on your desk by three this afternoon, Bob"*) to
my recently acquired children (*"Sure, Betsy, just make sure
you're back by ten"*), I was by greeted and treated with
the same convinced matter-of-fact respect that had been

rightly accorded my predecessor. Not once did someone look at me askance. Not once did anyone furrow their brow or rub their chin. Not once was I asked if I was feeling off-color and if I would like to sit down and be brought a nice glass of water. Nobody in fact seemed the slightest bit aware of the, quite frankly, cataclysmic substitution that had taken place right under their noses. Nobody seemed to suspect that when they now spoke to Bob T. Hash III, they were in reality conversing with a nearly six-foot-tall African gray parrot with a crimson-tipped tail.

Without having ever formulated it to myself, then, in any explicit punch-in-the-air, rung-gained, mirror-glancing, whoop-inducing, high-fiving kind of way, it seemed I'd been fast-track promoted, in one fell swoop, from the position of picture book avian mascot to fulcrum tycoon. For the first day or two of my new existence—laying aside for a moment any romantic complications with Matilda—I was content to trundle along the grooves of Bob T.'s routines, to roll along with events, with little thought of any long-term implications, and simply wait for whatever surprises the cuttlebone and fate had up their sleeves. I would not have been surprised, for example, if during those early days the magical effects of the cuttlebone had with little warning simply worn off, obliging me to return, perhaps at the most inconvenient and embarrassing of moments—need I say more—to my perch. Nor would I have been entirely flabbergasted to see teamleader™ Bob himself pop up again in grammar book Belmont. But the more time went by, the more it looked like whatever biochemical gestalt flip had taken place was this time firmly rooted, and the more I could take my human incarnation for granted. And, equally, the more time passed, the less likely it seemed big loser Bob would be returning to picture book Belmont.

The person with whom I might have anticipated the trickiest situations vis-à-vis the cataclysmic substitution, namely Matilda, seemed, if anything, to detect an actual *improvement* in her marital situation—though, fortunately, without this raising any alarm bells regarding the flush synchronicity between the vanishing and apparently defenestrated Comenius and the improvement in question. I should point out that Matilda and I had always had a bit of a soft spot for each other, back from my days as a parrot—so it was perhaps not surprising that my relationship with her would turn out to be the most real and, for want of a better word, the most human relationship that I was to form in my new incarnation. She confided to me—me now being her husband—how greatly her marriage in all aspects had lately improved. "It's like we're newlyweds again," she declared. The great tenderness and passion with which I so generously nursed Mrs. Hash through her parrot bereavement was, I believe, an important factor in shortening that bereavement, and in softening her very terrible loss.

It was in the delicate matrimonial matter of biblical mating especially that I might have expected to face the most nuanced, most sensitively charged tests of my emulatory talents. And, lo and behold, I found myself undergoing such a test on my first full night in Bob's shoes (perhaps I should say slippers), the origin and seed of which—its genesis—was that famous peck after dinner. Not having ever seen my host and hostess at congress, I had, of course, no template to follow. Nor was this the breeding season for parrots. Notwithstanding these terrible handicaps, I that night, in Matilda's own words, introduced into the department of sheet an "injection of thrill and a new lease on life." If a test of my emulatory talents this was, I had passed—no, I had *surpassed* the test—and with flying colors. It is a well-known fact that the parrot (along with a number of other but inferior species of bird) is both an honorable and a monogamous coupler.

Romantic things aside, my suspicions were growing that something altogether much fishier was going on with that grammarian's manuscript than I'd first imagined. Not only did the warped errata fail to fizzle out, as I'd been hoping, they seemed if anything to be getting worse. As *Forward with English!* indeed made its forward progress—rising like a glass-and-chrome mall escalator from the basic rudiments, up through the various levels of proficiency toward the shining Advanced Certificate—far from disappearing, the bizarrities just got wilder, more insistent, attaining new heights of scramble. What on my first day at the office I had taken charitably to be the as-yet-unculled flaws (due to the pressures of some in-house publishing deadline or a sloppy printer's glitches?) on subsequent days looked more likely the result of deliberate, not to say mischievous, tinkering. By the Vocabulary for Beginners section, tinkering had already reached chronic proportions.

There, on the surface of things, the prospective student is being invited to limber up with some light calisthenics. By invoking universally recognized household objects (all rather tellingly orphaned bric-a-brac from the Hash dwelling-of-residence), by employing a deceptively conventional format, and by disguising himself as a lexical midwife, the thus-far anonymous but suspiciously Bob T. Hash III–like compiler seems to be hoping to lull the learner into a state of passive receptivity. The planetary metaphors, the almost hallucinogenic insistence on color, and the entirely gratuitous preference for the indefinite article, however, should put us on the alert—for God-knows-what ribald acrobatics to come.

The question was: What did the Bob Hash I thought I had known—champion of the stock phrase, purveyor of lite-speak—have this unwarranted mumbo jumbo sitting on his desk for in the first place? Absconding from the picture book like a romantic Gauguin is one thing; mixing with malefactors who wish to throw mud at the unimpeachable picture world of Acme is another. Could it be I was discovering a playful, if not downright seditious, side to the man? Could it be that Bob had even himself taken a hand in their composition?

"Goodness to Betsy," I said out loud to myself, banging my fist on the desk (I was back in the office). "Hash *can't* be the prankster!"

12

Buying a Newspaper

In this skit, the student has to imagine that a business colleague has not been seen for a number of days. The situation becomes more serious when the missing colleague fails to turn up at an important meeting where he was due to present last quarter's sales figures. To find out the very latest developments, the concerned student goes to the newsstand for a newspaper to check over the missing persons list and obituary sections.

STUDENT: A *New York Times,* please, Bert.

VENDOR (doffing cloth cap): Sorry, Miss. We don't stock *The New York Times.*

STUDENT: Well, then, I'll take a *Washington Post.*

VENDOR: We don't stock that one either.

STUDENT: You wouldn't stock the *Belmont Gazette,* by any chance?

VENDOR: I'll just have a look. (Sounds of rustling from under the kiosk counter.) Yes (peering at date), here's today's edition of the *Belmont Gazette*!

STUDENT: Okay. I'll take the *Belmont Gazette,* please.

VENDOR: That'll be sixty cents.

STUDENT: Oh (on impulse) . . . and I'll take a Cuban cigar too, please.

VENDOR: That'll be one dollar fifty, Miss Scarlett.

STUDENT (handing him two crisp dollar bills): Just keep the change!

(CASH REGISTER: *ching-ching!*)

VENDOR: Much obliged, Miss Scarlett. (Doffs cap again profoundly.)

13

And there might have ended my involvement in the matter: Comenius the mascot African gray parrot returned, serene as a guardian angel, to his perch, the manuscript tucked back into its manila envelope and returned to the out tray, Matilda a waving widow on the veranda—if it weren't for the fact that I appeared to now be actually *trapped* in the role of Bob T. Hash III. Not that Bob's role was disagreeable in itself—I had after all tried very hard to get aboard a human adventure like this in the first place. I had learned how to open windows and doors. I had thrown my own Frisbee. I had driven Bob's car to the office and attended to the quarterly sales figures. Plus, of course, there was the serendipitous boon of being able to mate, as freely, with as much abandon, and as often as I wished, with his wife.

But as the extent of the damage done to the new course book material came to light, as did the perhaps less than innocent role that Bob had played in that damage, might not I one fine day be accused of those very scramblings myself?

Initially I had supposed my own species-flipping might take the same seesawing format as in *The Strange Case of Dr. Jekyll and Mr. Hyde,* with the cuttlebone playing the part of villainous toxin. And now, well, short of that, it would be nice to at least have the option of being able to flip out if things were to become too complicated in due course. I discovered that the metamorphosis was this time irreversible, and that that option was alas to be denied me!

Meanwhile, any remaining hopes that Bob had himself been unaware of the distortions taking place inside the new *Forward with English!* were pretty much dashed by a phone call I received in my office at eleven o'clock on the first Thursday morning of my new job. It was Mr. Gleason, the printer's assistant. In a barely audible voice Mr. Gleason was asking what had happened to the "package" that I—that is, Bob T. Hash III—had promised to send. "It hasn't arrived yet, and we're getting worried it's been lost in the mail," he said. "By the way, that last crop of crazy infringements you sent takes the cake!" I resisted the impulse to get annoyed with Mr. Gleason and ask him what in the devil's name was this "package" of crazy cake-taking infringements he was talking about. Quick-thinkingly, literally leaping ahead in terms of the plot pace and, in a voice as steady as I could manage, I told Mr. Gleason that, on a late rereading of my work, I (that is Bob T. Hash III) had decided to hang on to the manuscript for a few days longer in order to make some last-minute adjustments. I assured him that the moment it was ready I would have it FedEx-ed over to him.

"No problem, Mr. Hash," whispered Mr. Gleason. "Do bear in mind the master printer will be coming back from leave in a fortnight. If you want to get this stuff through unchecked then you'll have to get a move on."

I recradled the receiver, and tried to remain calm. I picked up the framed photo from the desk and tried to square the familiar image of the bland-browed businessman in his stolid thick-rimmed Clark Kent glasses and weekend cardigan in front of the veranda, with an emerging, and quite different profile altogether. I felt a very large penny drop inside me. It made a satisfying, old-fashioned *kedge-jing-click* sound.

One evening a few weeks before this, I remember Bob announcing that he had received a commission to compile the new eighth edition of *Forward with English!*—"That's wonderful,

darling!"—the seventh being deemed threadbare, pallid, dog-
eared, and in urgent need of an update. As popular protagonist,
fulcrum, and trustworthy citizen of the then current seventh
edition, Bob would have been the natural candidate for the
task. All he'd really have to do would be to pluck a few examples
from his daily routines, throw in a few rudimentary observations about the people around him, switch around a few names
here and there, throw in a few token concessions to the advances in technology and prevailing moral fashions, and leave
it to the picture book artist to refurbish the furniture and give
the white picket fences a fresh lick of paint.

   That same evening after dinner, I had watched him sit down
at his living room desk to embark on the task, apparently with
no motive ulterior than dispatching a competent, regular grammar book to the specifications the update required. After a few
days of an initial and enthusiastic drafting, however, Bob's
work pace began to slow down. It began with some idle doo-
dlings in the margins. Innocent enough, you will say—the
emarginated juxtaposition of his *"This is a table, this is a chair"*
with a badly drawn three-dimensional hexagon, or his *"Someone has left a banana peel under the window"* coupled with a
haywirish galaxy spiral. Next thing, scrunched-up sheets of
discarded paper began to brim from the proverbial—and albino
cornucopial—wastebasket (*Br. Eng.: "bin"*). You knew then that
something was wrong. Bob looked bored, an impression not
helped by his perching his previously swashbuckling chin on
upturned palms, elbows resting on the evening desktop. And
well might he be. The very act of writing down the routines and
phrases from his life revealed to him what can only be described
as the *stultifying banality* contained therein, to which he had
hitherto been—astonishingly—purblind. I watched him from
my various perches growing annoyed at himself for having ac-
cepted Acme's drudgely commission. As an aspiring man of
letters he felt chained to the humdrum—but worse was the re-
alization that his plan to embezzle from Acme—subsequently
abandoned—and run off with his secretary who as we know

turned out to be the lascivious Miss Scarlett—subsequently executed—might now by the clay feet of his progress, or lack thereof, on the updated eighth edition of *Forward with English!,* be put into jeopardy.

It was time to pull out the finger (*see* Idiomatic Expressions) from that stagnant becalming, and get on with his course book. Finish the course book first, then the elopement: no reason given why Bob might have things in that order—other than a congenital dash of good old-fashioned work ethic (*see* Hobbies and Pastimes). And that it lets us ratchet in a bit of motivation on the old plot front—which so far holds about as much water as an episode of *Commissioner Rex,* about an Alsation dog that's convinced it's Sherlock Holmes.

Bob had arrived at the conclusion—a kind of purple epiphany—that the only way he would be able to resume the project at all was by composing not just one but *two* versions of *Forward with English!* and to work on them in tandem. As per the terms of the commission, he would continue to work on the original version, which had thus far only instilled in him that heightened sense of ubiquitous absurdity. But, alongside that version, he would now also compose a *second* version parallel to the first that, thanks to its indeed Joycean tidbit and free-jazz exuberance, would act as a kind of lightning conductor for his fresh existential insight—thus neutralizing any sense of disaffection that the first version gave him and thus allow him to finish in time for his scheduled elopement with Miss Scarlett. He would submit the regular innocuous version to be published (as the eighth edition) keeping this second one aside for his own private amusement—and that way keep himself sane.

I remember seeing a documentary about Christopher Columbus, the great explorer, on the living room TV. Apparently, on his voyage across the Atlantic, Columbus had kept two ship's logbooks, not just one. He'd had one logbook that charted the actual progress of his vessels across the ocean, which he kept locked up and away from the superstitious eyes of his crew, who might break into mutiny should the ships' true trajectory be disclosed. He had a second logbook too, in which he plotted a course showing his ships to never have strayed out of safe charted waters, and so placated his shipmates. What, I now wondered, if Bob had used a similar ruse himself?

As his two versions of *Forward with English!* progressed, so pleased must he have been with his own private version that at a certain point Bob must have decided it was actually *better* than the original version, the one that adhered to the terms of the commission. The little demon on his shoulder, with its tiny cartoon devil's trident, like a pirate's mad bad parrot, was gaining his ear. And on its advice Bob came to defenestrate (*to throw out the window*) any notion of Hippocratic oath for compilers of grammar course–type books: he'd get his own warped-out version of *Forward with English!* into print instead!

In its various phases, Bob would let Acme's publisher see some fragment of the so-called regular, or decoy version. More important, by sending off fragments of the canonical primer for approval, he was able to build up between himself and the master printer a bond of trust—while at the same time he could sound out which of the master's assistants was perhaps amenable to corruption. Now and again Bob would slip in the odd sample of his apocryphal version to see if anyone would notice. In many ways it resembled the canonical original—in the same way Columbus's logbook would have looked very much like the true version—employing the same basic, verisimilitudinous format, only distorted through the prism of Bob's perverted imagination. At first he'd slipped in just a page or two to get the green light, but by now having brokered a little deal with Mr. Gleason, Bob was able to submit ever larger sections of his bogus version, his *darkly comic* Pandora's proofs, without an eyelid being batted. In this, fragments of the original illustrative example from the canonical version still showed through like a resilient palimpsest. Model exercises of sober practicality in the orthodox grammar book, tourist-guide-style, only now overlaid with Bob's zany and ever more elaborate incursions and miscreant spannerisms. This was no mere sprinkling of playful forgeries—but sabotage on an industrial scale!

The enormity—the ingeniousness!—of the whole business was now beginning to dawn on me. That elopement in large part was a smoke screen, timed to coincide with the master printer's absence, leaving corrupt minion Mr. Gleason in charge. On its eve the by-now-dastardly Bob was able to slip into his out tray the vandalized entirety, that Trojan horse twin, in the knowledge that it would pass through the printers unchallenged.

All this, of course, had serious implications for my own situation. For soon there was going to be trouble—for Mr. Bob T. Hash III—on account of those pernicious corruptions. That is if they weren't removed before somebody found them.

I put that framed photo of the Hashes in front of their veranda that I'd picked up at the start of this chapter back on the desk and resolved to come to the rescue of *Forward with English!*

At the Dry Cleaners: Taking Things in Your Stride!

In a previous skit, student discovered a rather nasty stain on his jacket, most likely an ink stain from a leaking pen, though he did have suspicions it was something more sinister, such as blood. At the end of the skit, student left the jacket at the dry cleaners, who assured him that the stain would indeed be removed. It is now Thursday afternoon and time for the student to return to the shop to see if the dry cleaner has lived up to his word.

> (DRY CLEANER DRYLY CONSULTING STUB; CHIEF PROTAGONIST REMAINING MUTE, INCIPIENT AGHASTNESS): "Yes, sir, the stain came out beautifully. However, I think you'll find you already collected your jacket this morning."

Having decided to set myself up as troubleshooter to the orphaned grammar, the first thing was to devise a working
method and to sort out my basic approach. I decided the best
thing was to divide the task into two distinct phases. The aim of
the first, *Forward with English!* phase one, was to clear the
ground. Clearly, before I could begin to turn things around, I
was going to have to get rid of the virus intrusions by
eliminating all traces of the saboteur's regurgitated
squib. Even that first morning at the desk in Bob's executive office, casually flicking through the manuscript, without
really knowing what I was reading yet, my pen had more than
once instinctively leaned in toward the more glaring errata,
itching to score out the prankster's nascent tidbit. As editor in
chief, I needed now restrain my censor's pencil no longer. In the
many free hours I had at my disposal in the office, I now began
sifting through the material, teasing out anything untoward
that might prove confusing to the student, making ample use of
the little Wite-Out brush (just like the one for Matilda's nail
varnish). I removed the titanic typos. I jettisoned the hokum
outcries and outré pokum. I showed politely but firmly to the
door the "all-Greek-to-me"s. I sniffed out like verbal truffles the
oases of claptrap, winnowed out the drunken glitches, extirpated the carbuncular bunkum, expunged the archipelagos of
bafflement, shepherded the pyrotechnics off to the side,
and excised the beachheads of baroqueries and engib-

berated potpourrificatory errata—to leave a scaled-down but most sensible rump in their stead.

It is on the foundations of this sensible rump that the revised version of the eighth edition of *Forward with English!* has been reconstituted, in a no less valiant phase two, wherein the eliminated bric-a-brac has been replaced with their down-to-earth bright dinky cousins. In the composition of replacements I have commandeered material from a range of sources. Armed now always with a notebook and pencil, I jotted down fieldwork notes from the hundred bright little routine eventlets that made up the mortal days of Bob T. Hash III—anything from the wording of everyday greetings (*"Great to see you again, Janet!"*) to the purchasing procurement procedure for a silk-lined narrow-brim brown-felt Sinatra-style fedora hat with its ribbon and its infamous dimpled crown. In the office canteen I would interview colleagues. At mini-conferences I would hand out little informal questionnaires. Staff newsletters and trade magazines also came in handy. I have been able to cite a multitude of Bob's own Formica-surfaced clipped-together stock phrases retained in my parrot's memory.

In addition, I had at my disposal a glossy protocopy of the proposed eighth edition of the accompanying pictures, to which the written sections make copious references, and which of course remained immune to Bob's nefarious graffiti. Please note that in several pictures, like a saint in a fresco, Bob can appear more than once, but do not be alarmed. Here he is, for example, getting his hair trimmed at Harry the barber's—while through the barber's window in the same picture you see him buying a newspaper from Bert at the newsstand. In another picture, you see Bob, after a morning's industrious toil, standing in line at the staff canteen—look carefully and you can see him on his way out, stacking his empty tray. In another, Bob's at the department store in Belmont purchasing a new trilby, but at the same time at a background counter of the same store he's returning a defective pair of cuff links. In another, he's taking his wife out to the theatre—but only two rows behind them he's sharing an industrial-size bucket of popcorn with Miss Scarlett. In yet another, Bob's on the golf course—but that's not Bert on the tractor mowing in the background, it's Bob T. Hash III in dungarees and rolled-up lumberjack shirtsleeves.

My aim, throughout all aspects of this task, was to be as unobtrusive an editor as possible. My guiding principle was to reinvest Bob's out tray apocrypha with as much as possible of what I imagined to be the core spirit of the original "decoy" version (which a subsequent search of both living room and office desks failed, alas, to unearth). In my parrot phase, I had already absorbed—by osmosis, no doubt—the very ethos of anodyne melaminity so central to the course book, in its original form. This meant that in my role as editor I was able to remain true to the spirit of the bland, stalwart captain of industry before he misplaced his marbles and began tampering around with the wires of his own creation. Far from trying to supplant or outshine my predecessor's original efforts, I hope to have left them as much as possible intact, for which Bob should even now still take the bulk of the credit.

Repairs and Rectifications

Bob T. Hash III sat on a wall
Bob T. Hash III had a great fall
All the king's horses and all the king's men
Couldn't put Bob T. Hash III together again.

A sling, a set of crutches, and a packet of nurses' Elastoplast bandages may be provided by teacher.

How close Bob came to getting away with his fiendish plan! How nearly civilization as we know it almost drew to a standstill. But for my timely actions, his dastardly, demented *Forward with English!* might have passed through the printers without so much as a spell-check, to be churned out like hotcakes and distributed to the four corners of the globe. Millions and millions of unwitting would-be Bob T. Hash IIIs would at this very moment be organizing meetings, managing projects, conducting workshops, all babbling away in Bob's new whacked-out lite-speak—and not an eyebrow would be raised.

Meanwhile, in the turquoise shade of a pool of some highrise hotel in Acapulco, Bob was chortling into his rum and Coke, saluting a bamboo umbrella. . . .

Imperatives

The uniquely formulated and breakthrough Acme Philosophy™ is based on learning through practical example, and is scientifically proven to optimize the student's success.

Some typical examples:
(i)   Keep off the Astroturf!
(ii)   Mind you don't fall out of that window!
(iii)   Jump through the hoop, please!
(iv)   Stop the gondola here, gondolier. My wife wants an ice.
(v)   Let the Egg and Pie World Championship commence!
(vi)   Knees bent, left arm straight, eye on the ball, pat down the divot.
(vii) Sitzen Sie bitte.
(viii) Pedal faster the bright peals of laughter.
(ix)   Don't let me ever see you near this pet shop again, d'you hear!

Student might like to think about who these might be said by, under what circumstances, and to whom in each case they might be addressed. Now match up the letters with their Latinate numerical equivalents. The answers have been done already in order to help you.

a) golfer's resolute injunction to pre-swing zen-mastering self (vi)

b) cantankerous picnicking Astroturf salesman to blind man wandering astray from leisure park pea stone (i)

c) at the Düsseldorfian equivalent of the London Crufts dog show, addressed to a shepherd (vii)

d) to chortling mono-cyclist (viii)

e) to circus acolyte trainee walrus-cum-student (iii)

f) arriving exuberantly at Ye Olde Egg and Pie Shop (v)

g) to a light-bathed maid of Vermeer (or de Hooch) (ii)

h) to Italianate punter passing quayside "gelateria," bride in need of her magnum (iv)

i) to incompetent air-conditioning maintenance man on threshold of pet shop (ix)

LANGUAGE TIP! Student should bear in mind that imperatives (or even pseudo-imperatives) don't necessarily have to be issued by Bob T. Hash III in person. Naturally, when an imperative is uttered by Bob T. Hash III (or by one of his proxies), it takes on an added air of authority perhaps lacking in other speakers. But while Bob does bob up rather frequently in the picture book, he is not technically speaking omnipresent and cannot be on hand whenever, and wherever, an order needs to be given. As a general rule, therefore, imperatives not lucky enough to be uttered by Bob should command our attention notwithstanding: if something needs to be done with any urgency, there is little point in waiting around for Bob to come along and dish out instructions. By the time he gets round, it might well be too late.

19

Not long after I began my sober bowdlerized revisions of the material for the new and improved eighth edition of *Forward with English!* (with the odd advertisement thrown in for good measure), I thought it might not be a bad idea to supply some kind of section-by-section commentary on Bob's hoax versions (here presented)—if only to demonstrate the many great improvements I have made and, where appropriate, to give credit yet to Bob.

By the way, if now and again some supporting non-Bob characters from picture book Belmont give us a sense of déjà vu, this is because we probably *have* seen them before. The Acme budget can feed and clothe and house only the most prominent citizens of Belmont—the ones who get speech bubbles and get lines in the exercises. To make up numbers for things like conference applause settings, fire drill debouchments, mall complex scenes, etc. (life-size cycloramas of *Where's Waldo?* or, more accurately, *Where's Bob T. Hash III?*), hack extras get bused in from out of town. This kind of work is by nature precarious and seasonal, forcing not only picture book extras but sometimes regulars too to supplement their income by putting in hack appearances in glossy catalogues—in any case never more than a stone's throw from our own pastel incunabula. Steve Winshaw, for example, seemingly rooted to the petty accounts desk in the picture book office, was the stubble-chinned cowboy from last summer's *Interiors* catalogue, seen lounging on a clip-together chaise longue teaching his daughter the rudiments of chess. Before she took on the more permanent role as my replacement PA, Miss Happ appeared in last spring's bumper edition of *Good Housekeeping,* in a cheesecloth frock, skipping through a ripe purple field of lavender in the south of France. Sally from public relations is perhaps more famous for shaving a well-toned calf on the pink slender rim of a luxury bathtub in an advertisement for faucets, parrot stand in the corner of her bathroom.

Talking of parrot stands, I had better describe what happened to mine. As you already know, on my first fateful afternoon as torch-bearing Bob I had assisted Matilda in its postcalamity reconstruction. Once more assembled, it was returned to its habitual position by the living room window, pristine and patient. For a number of days, with tenderness and care, both seed tray and water were replenished to keep them looking fresh; the rungs of the ladder were dusted to keep them spick-and-span; the mirror polished to keep its reflections free from smudges. It all looked very inviting, I must say! But as the days rolled on, reality began to sink in.

As hope that Comenius would return began to wane, attention to seed tray and water was replaced by unforeseen passions. With moves choreographed to the positional logic of grief, the cage began its slow but inevitable retreat. It was initially transferred (supposedly on a temporary basis) to the rear of the couch where it suddenly seemed more convenient—but alas, not quite convenient enough. Next thing, like a receding phantom, the stand was pushed farther back still, looming for a few days in the living room corner. From whence it was then shunted into the hall, where it was subsequently deemed an impediment to the free flow of pedestrian traffic.

Finally, one rainy weekend, the entire apparatus was quietly dismantled. The seed tray was emptied, the sawdust was cleaned out from the base of the cage, the accoutrements were wrapped up in sheets of the *Belmont Gazette*. The disparate sections were then withdrawn from service to a windowless cupboard that was located under the stairs.

"Brand Loyalty"—An Advertisement for the Institute!

Thank you for choosing to learn your second language with Acme! To supplement your classroom instruction, a wide range of "state-of-the-art" audiovisual cassettes and interactive CD-ROMs are available from the front desk. Ideal for home study programs or for use in our high-tech language lab facilities, these materials form an extension of our fully integrated program of business-oriented course books. Constantly updated through rigorous in-house product testing, all our products are specially tailored to the demanding challenges of the contemporary parrot's busy international lifestyle and reflect our ongoing commitment to patent protection. For the fast-track goal-orientated cosmopolitan business supremo and ambitious professional alike, our products are a must. (Logofied key rings, coffee mugs, wall calendars, and fluffy toys for small impressionable children are also available. Just ask at the desk.)

—That's rather expensive, is it not?
—Don't look at it as a cost, Jack. Just think of it as an investment in your future!

By "parrot" as in the phrase "demanding challenges of the contemporary parrot's busy international lifestyle," Bob is presumably referring to the *Psittacus erithacus*—more commonly known, and with understandably widespread popular affection, as the African gray parrot. And, despite his nefarious meddlings in the matter of the manila I cannot help but feel a little flattered—as I proceed with my sectional commentaries—that such a renowned and authoritative compiler of course manuals should, in his otherwise astringent pageantry of lozenged examples, find the time and space to allude to that humble bird of which I am indeed an exemplar. How easy it would have been, when describing today's busy international lifestyle, for Bob to have alluded instead to any number of lesser feathered aviators: to the mariner's albatross, for example; to the immaculate dove returning from a distant shore with its sprig of quaint foreign expression; to the magpie with a shining literary tidbit in its beak; or to the miner's yellow canary (snuffing it, as with noxious gas, in the presence of impish interpolation); or again to the noble ostrich, with its head in the sand—not to mention the cuckoo, the jay, the nightingale, the godwit, the mockingbird, the stonechat, the warbler, the secretary bird, the puffin, the hummingbird . . . or to any one of a no doubt infinite variety of tits.

On the other hand, given that history is chockablock with examples of illustrious parrots, parrot is maybe not as surprising a choice as you might at first think. Kept as domestic companions and confidants by the great and the good, in their castles and boudoirs, in the very citadels of modern democracy, that's parrots for you. African grays in particular have been prized for their gift as affable mimics, and in that capacity have so often been privy to the inner thoughts of the "makers and shakers" of their day. What key event that has shaped the destinies of civilizations has *not* been attended upon by the African gray? What pretty stenographer does not daily think of how Columbus brought back for Isabella of Spain a magnificent pair of Cuban Amazons? What photocopying apprentice worth her salt does not dream at night of how Henry VIII, who kept a parrot at Hampton Court, was one day saved by it with a well-timed imperative from drowning in the river? What motel chambermaid doesn't think of wise King Solomon's sage bird, or of Casanova's popinjay when she's making one's bed up? What Russian princess doesn't slaver Slavically at the thought of Anastasia and her nice pair of Jacos? What lusty intern doesn't remember how President Roosevelt kept an African gray in the White House? What saloonstress of letters can forget how Dorothy Parker's Onan spilled its stain on her chintzes? Alexander the Great, Queen Victoria, Winston Churchill, all inevitably had their parrots—and who knows what wise counsel they received from them during moments of national crisis!

And little wonder that such a luminous bird should find itself in the picture manual's protagonist's front living room, or leading a busy international lifestyle.

Over and above this justified homage to the species, please note the nod of personal gratitude (probably inadvertent) in anticipation of the efforts I myself would one day expend in rescuing this snippet, in slim-lining it down, for the purposes of fruitful instruction.

Nevertheless, both here and in the eventuality of any sort of situation of mortal combat that might arise in the future, Professor Bob would do well to remember that flattery will get him nowhere, will get him nowhere at all.

22

Summer Courses Abroad— Another Advertisement!

Congratulations for reaching this important milestone in your course! Now that you've made such great progress, why not continue your studies by attending one of our special summer courses abroad? Pick up the accent of your choice. Live as a local as part of native-speaking households with our in-board accommodation teaching vacations, available in a wide range of exciting locations:

- *spend a rhyming slang fortnight within earshot of the bells of Saint Clemens in a household of genuine pearly-button waist-coated Dickensian Cockneys*
- *take to the sea in galoshes and yellow oilskin with a packet of anti-seasick pills and a shoal of Aberdonian fishermen and then return home to impress your friends and colleagues with the soft incomprehensibilities of the local dialect*
- *share early morning milk duties and pick up a West*

Country accent with a family of teat-squeezing Devon-
shire dairy farm milkmaids

• *spend a drawling month among Texan oil tycoons and*
  add a swagger to your outlook

• *drink beer "straight from the can" and learn that old*
  billabong outback backpackin' dingbat surf-speak
  around the campfire with Skippy and the Bluey Bush
  Ranchers on the slopes of Ayers Rock . . . and much, much
  more!

But perhaps you wish to eliminate that nasty regional accent? Time to get rid of those annoying glottal stops? Time to
BOTOX those vowels, bowdlerize your vocabulary? Why not
come to an English south-coast Balbec for estuary schoolmarm
and scones at the Acme-Ashley Institute? Summer courses to
suit all needs, with prim sea views and garden path gnomes.
Traditional hospitality provided at Mrs. Widow-Smith's guest-
house (curfew at 10:00 p.m.). Faded esplanade tearooms and
crayons for rainy afternoons with views of the pavilion.

23

As my editorial work on the course sections began to gather pace, I became aware of a desire to share the story of Comenius's metamorphosis—unlikely as it was that anyone would ever believe me, to say nothing of putting my revision work on *Forward with English!* at risk—but it was simply too big, too incredible a story to keep under my trilby. I amused myself by formulating different, almost novelistic, ways I might tell it, thinking of the different angles, inventing a town and a few minor characters to act as a backdrop. The time sequence bit was not going to be easy. I would have to choose an accent—as per the advertisement above. I could stick in an Ovid, I could stick in a *Commissioner Rex.*

This desire to relate my little tale was particularly strong, of course, in regard to Matilda; I wanted very much to watch the play of incredulity, of laughter, on her face—*darling, you must be pulling my leg!*—while I spun my homespun wordsmithly phrases. Yet despite her intelligent laughter and healthy ser-endipitously un–*Forward with English!* cynicism, I wasn't quite sure even Matilda was ready to appreciate learning the ornithologically related fact that she was conjugally conjoined to a parrot. On my own account, I'd have had no qualms—look, here's my crimson-tipped tail! But on account of the sanity of *Forward with English!* the risk was still just too great. It was best I bide my time till *Forward with English!* was in the clear. . . .

I take it as understood, by the way, that as I work my way through the manila material, I am still doing all those regular, ordinary, air-conditioned day-to-day things that Bob did. I get up every morning at a quarter to seven, I wash, I have breakfast, I drive to the office, I open the mail, I answer the phone, I chair this, I signature that. I read Laurie Lee and listen to Charlie Parker. I mow the lawn on the weekends and play Frisbee with the children. (I've even been away on a business trip of my own!) I also take it as understood that Matilda has *her* own parallel set of day-to-day things: when she isn't with me it's not like—well, it's not simply that she's absent, floating about in some big tub of aspic in a bikini. She's doing things all of the time, as real as I'm writing this sentence. You can see what she's up to now, just look at page 34 of the picture book: Matilda setting the table for breakfast. Matilda at the mall. Matilda in her motor car on the way to the mall. Matilda at the ladies' hairdressers, her hair wrapped up in tinfoil under the hood of a bubblegum-pink dryer . . .

That's where I found her, head under the bubblegum hood, when, succumbing one day to a mad lunchtime impulse, I ducked out of the office canteen, gripped by the idea of going directly to Matilda to tell her the true fate of Comenius. It was an impetuous, crazy idea. Part of me of course realized that it would probably have been better to wait till Matilda and I were alone in the evening, say curled up on the couch with a test card in the living room after the children had gone off to bed. But I was flushed from a successful morning's editing and felt that my sheer enthusiasm would override any absurdities of making a full-blown public announcement at the ladies' hairdressers' in broad Belmont daylight.

When I put my head through the hairdressers' door and doffed my fedora, several pairs of ladies' eyes looked up at me, surprised to see an unscheduled man there—an unscheduled Bob T. Hash III, at that. Nice big (bell-less) mirrors above a row of gleaming porcelain sinks, I noticed. On shelves, lotions: unction and herbal—often with squirting devices attached. The place smelled of hair stuff and perfume. Miss Ting at the cash register, her coin drawer ajar. Miss Snip, frozen midsnip with her scissors paused slicing the air. Janet, from accounts, getting a nice seventies wavy perm done for an upcoming drinks do at the office. Matilda was watching me in the mirror, strands of waxy tinfoil poking out from the sides of the noisy hood. On her lap, in a magazine, Doris Day and James Garner were embracing each other in a scene from an old movie I'd watched from a rainy afternoon's perch. In it, Doris Day's first husband, played by a pre–*Rockford Files* James Garner, had been in a plane crash. Presuming him dead—please pass the popcorn—Doris remarries a millionaire schmuck in order to continue her life of diamonds and glamour to which she was accustomed (*see* Habits). The twist in the film, a very early twist in the film at any rate, is that pre-*Rockford* Garner hasn't perished at all—his plane has only ditched into the ocean. He's been washed up on a Pacific island, replete with pineapples and coconut skirts. After a few years of pineapples and coconut skirts, Rockford escapes from the island, as from the Island of Circe, and next thing, like a spruced-up Robinson Crusoe, he just happens to bump into Doris in a swanky hotel lobby while husband number two is off sorting out the luggage with the bellhop (*"Right away, Sir. Fifth floor it is!"*). The stage is set for some light afternoon farce. More fumbling suitcase and wardrobe regurgitation than nasty shoot-outs or duels but, nevertheless, just seeing the photo there on Matilda's lap, I couldn't help feeling there were perhaps certain parallels with my own situation: inversions, mirrorings, coincidences; certain possible slapstick developments that, in my impetuous resolution, I'd perhaps not quite thought through yet. Was Bob for example, as gone for good as I'd imagined? Had I not been maybe unwittingly cast in a role similar to that millionaire schmuck, shunted off to the side of the stage—the wings—with the suitcases?

As I neared Matilda's chair (her eyes following me in the mirror with a mischievous expression on her face), I was already retracting my idea of telling her my story of psittacine resurrection. No, I resolved: the time is not nigh yet. Matilda's hood dryer was switched on, as if by an invisible hand. It was quite loud, and it would have been difficult to hear ourselves speak.

24

Aloud vs. Loudly

"Loudly" is used to indicate an emphatic impression upon the tympanum. It is the adverbial form of the adjective "loud," used to register a relatively elevated level of decibel. "Loud" can also be used to describe clothing, colors, persons, etc. The opposite of "loudly" is "quietly."

Examples:
- He mowed the lawn loudly.
- The gun made a loud bang when the man pulled the trigger.
- Did you see that loud dress Mrs. Thompson was wearing at the party?
- There was snow; he doffed his hat quietly.
- I'M A GREAT GUY is so loud—will someone please turn him down!
- The hairdresser turned off the hood dryer. It was too loud to hear yourself think.

"Aloud" is sometimes used with words such as "think" and "read" to say that words are actually spoken using the vocal apparatus, often with a view to being heard, as opposed to having words just wheeling around inside someone's head as fragments of some inner narrative. Something can be said aloud but at almost a whisper; conversely, someone can have a very loud, almost deafening, and perhaps very interesting narrative going on in their head, entirely inaudible to persons around them, standing perhaps only inches away.

"Goodness to Betsy," I said aloud to myself, banging my fist on the office desk. "Hash can't be the prankster!"

25

I was approaching the hairdresser's mirror. There was a very interesting narrative going on in my head entirely inaudible to persons around me, perhaps only inches away. Matilda's reflection was smiling at me, still following me with her eyes in the mirror. . . . Oh, but why was I fooling myself? What else had I come here for but a long cool draft of the flicker of mischief, of adventure, in those eyes? What did it matter if her fraud of a husband was dead, or if I'd once been a parrot; what difference would any of *that* make to our blossoming romance?

From the dryer, not a peep, not a breath of hot air: so quiet you could have heard a hair dryer drop. By way of explaining my presence (more for the benefit of the other ladies than for my wife, per se), I asked my wife—quite loudly—if she happened to know "where the car keys are," pretending to have mislaid them like Bobby with his recalcitrant satchel. This would have been immediately and immensely acceptable to all: a rational action man is in our midst. Matilda, however, her mind coming in from that different, almost Lady Macbethish angle I was telling you about, plucked a joke from the air and flung back the dryer. All at once she stood up and did a Betty Boop kick, all mock coquettish face and a hand to the back of her head. And then, as if that weren't enough, she puffed out her cheeks and started tugging at the bits of silver foil in her hair, moving her legs like a hospital clown wading through air made of aspic, or she was acting out that scene from the Late for a Train section with a "Doubting Thomas the Tank" pulling slowly away from the platform.

Barely divested of the hairdresser's trimmings, Matilda grabbed me by the hand; we ran outside the shop and skipped along Main Street.

With Matilda, Belmont had just turned into a big play park.

"Is that a blue car or a red car?"

We swung around lampposts.

"Where is the book?"

We tripped off curbs.

"I think that photocopier's out of order again, Dan."

We slow-motion leapfrogged over fire hydrants, laughing to the point of hysterics.

"I'll take the Belmont Gazette *and a packet of no-thanks-I-don't-smokes."*

(Like Lady Macbeth, Matilda was wearing a classy-broad split-side avocado green woolen skirt with matching cotton underpanties that flashed into view as she straddled the hydrants.)

But let's leave our amorous banterers to skip up Main Street alone; let's go back and have another look at the exercise while they're gone. That bit about turning down I'M A GREAT GUY for example. This in the original would of course have read *"Will someone please turn down BOB T. HASH III!"*—yet another instance of how a good slice of solid down-to-earth, no-nonsense, honest-to-goodness, toe-the-line, textbook grammar in the approved house style had become bastardized, and now lay in ruins.

In my version of *Forward with English!* you'll be relieved to know that the wrench has been removed from the gears, the long stem of a daisy has been inserted into the humorless barrel of an unflinching crew-cutted conscript's rifle. Yes, in the new eighth edition you'll find the sort of upbeat textbook stuff that our bespectacled Clark Kent, with his judicious admixture of pasteurized pre–phone box masculinity and quietly stated

picture book heroism, was made for. Emerging with that confident, chiseled oblongular jawline from his chrysalis phone
booth (lightly doffing trilby) striding forth to defend the integrity of an abused phrasal verb, to rescue the screaming
damsel from a burning mall inferno—and round up the maver-
ick polyglot prankster.

26

Delivering a Sales Pitch!

Construction engineers Bob and Jack are down on the site all hard hats and neckties, overseeing the work-in-progress on the new mall's foundation. We catch up with them taking an afternoon coffee break outside the foreman's trailer:

JACK: Say, Bob, I just took up Swahili lessons at that new language school they opened up on Main Street.

BOB: You mean that big glass-and-steel building located next to the bank, Jack?

JACK: That's the building, Bob, the big glass-and-steel one located next to the bank. I started lessons only a few weeks ago and already I can converse on a wide range of topics—effective marketing strategies, customer retention options, and so forth. My fluency maybe isn't perfect yet, but I'm sure working hard on bringing it up to the mark.

BOB (clearly impressed): Heck, Jack, that's impressive!

JACK (modestly): Well, I try my best, Bob. But really, if

anyone should take the credit, it's the folks who came up with the course material, and the instructors for their friendly dedication—good old-fashioned teamwork. Why don't you come along sometime? Learning can be fun, you know—and can do wonders for your career prospects. There's a great special offer on at the moment too!

BOB (debamboozled): You know, Jack, I've been meaning to take up Swahili for some time now and I just keep giving it the old rain check.

JACK (wistfully): I was the same, Bob. What with the pace of life these days, I felt there was just too much on my plate. But when I saw that ad campaign for Swahili lessons at the new school, I was able to make room in my busy schedule—and just look at me now. Randolf Crabtree says I'm in line for promotion!

BOB (back to basics): I saw that ad campaign too. What kind of price range are we talking here, Jack?

JACK: Well, Bob—no thanks, I don't take sugar—normally a three months' parrot intensive course for beginners will set you back in the region of a couple of thousand, but with this special offer on at the moment, you get a free professional assessment *plus* you get a bonus point discount option on course extension. Personally, I don't consider it so much an expense, Bob, as an investment in the future.

BOB: Hmm. That's an interesting way to think about it. And that special offer sounds just too good to miss out on. You know, Jack, I might just check out the options there, and see which one suits me best.

JACK: I knew you'd like the idea, Bob. I look forward to having some interesting conversations with you in Swahili in the not-too-distant future. And don't forget—

no thanks, I don't smoke—that special offer ends Friday, so be sure to enroll before then.

BOB (big Australian accent): No worries, Jack. I look forward to taking the challenge.

Jack and Bob whoop (high-five!) and return inside the portacabin to continue their work.

27

Talking of the challenges of today's busy international go-getting jet-setter lifestyle, has anyone here ever tried whooping and high-fiving a mirror's reflection? (The trick of course is to not actually slap the mirror.) A fascination with mirrors in general, the temptation to ascend short multicolored ladders—these impulses remained with me from my life as a parrot. Generally speaking, I observed mirrors in the human world to be rectangular, functional things, nowhere near as much fun as the little round one that used to hang on my cage, with its little bell and its little yellow border. Nevertheless, whenever I now see a mirror—the one in the office elevator for straightening your necktie, the row of looking glasses at the ladies' hairdressers, the wash basin mirror in the en suite bathroom where I first encountered the new improved Bob T. Hash III—my instinct is still to draw up close, now draw away, drawing nearer again, my head cocked over now onto one shoulder, now onto the other—not so much out of vanity as out of sheer amazement at the sight of Bob T. Hash III acting like a parrot in front of a mirror. And then for the sheer simple thrill of mirrors themselves. Similarly, ladders proved as difficult to resist in my guise as a human as they had done in my life as a parrot. A ladder with a reflection at its summit is going to be a rare and welcome conjunction indeed!

A day or two after the incident at the ladies' hairdressers, having put the final touches to the sales pitch (yet more raw material on that construction site for a future and burgeoning Everyday Accidents and Domestic Mishaps section), Miss Happ reminded me that it was time to pick up some duplicate snaps at the photographer's shop in the mall—just one of the many extracurricular tasklets that help flesh out Bob's workweek. I consulted my agenda and the wall clock behind me, and saw that Miss Happ was right. "Man the fort, Miss Happ," I said, throwing on my jacket.

At the photographer's shop, I gave the man in the white coat a tab and he passed me the snaps. I gave them a brief flick through to check they were not out of focus and paid the assistant ("No thanks, I won't be needing any enlargements"). I collected my negatives, tucked them inside my jacket, and walked out of the shop. Almost immediately, leaning against the plate glass window of the optician shop next door, I noticed a ladder. Someone must have put this up while I was going through the snaps. It was a window cleaner's Jacobian Ramsay, complete with (unpainted) aluminum rungs. It had rubber pads to stop it from slipping on the mall's smooth fake-marble floor. On a rung was draped a chamois rag, from which steam rose: again it was like the *Mary Celeste*. Like a sentry at its base stood a patient bucket of suds. I surmised that the cleaning man (or cleaning woman) had no sooner erected the thing than gone off for a coffee break. The ladder was unguarded, free for any passing Tom, Dick, or Harry to ascend it, should they so wish. . . .

A moment or so later, the kindly optician, Mr C. Good, came dashing out of his shop. Halfway up the ladder outside his window display was a man in an immaculately pressed (African) gray serge pin-striped business suit with crisp angled pleats, an enlogofied (but not yet clip-on) necktie, and some Brylcreem in his hair. Head cocked cheekily now to one shoulder, now to the other, the man appeared to be rocking toward his reflection in the window, withdrawing, then rocking forward again.

Very tactfully, very respectfully, with no hint of urgency or panic ("It's okay, Mr. Hash: You can come down now"), I was invited to descend, and to enter the optician shop for a leisurely browse. Of particular interest was a rack with a new range of frames, in the classic trademark Clark Kent style.

A Curious Encounter . . .

You run into someone unexpectedly on the vast vaulted airport concourse. You say:

a)   Small world!

b)   Off to Acapulco again, Bob?

c)   Small airport!

d)   Caramba! So it is you, Señor Gonzalez! And what might bring you to this neck of the woods?

e)   No, Bob, I think I'll just take a Greyhound.

f)   Ouch, what a stupid place to leave a mirror lying around!

g)   No, I think you must be thinking of somebody else.

h)   Ah, yes, it's all beginning to make sense now.

i)   Let's just say it's nice to have both feet back on the ground!

j)   These damn Windsors, Warren! You know, I've decided to invest in one of those newfangled clip-ons, after all!

The business of flying should be the preserve of creatures designed by God and by nature to do so—parrots, for example.

Habits and Habituation, Past and Present

To be/get used to (doing) something means that something is no longer new and strange to us and so no longer a strain on our attention. An inconvenient one-off uniqueness of vivid human encounter and experience, now neutralized and packaged, has been assimilated into the happy community of habit. Use of this form may denote a shift from foreground to background, from the visible to invisible. Do not confuse with "used to do something," or "used to be something" (nor, for that matter, with the instrumentalist's "used for," as in "that air-conditioning system is used for keeping the room cool").

Examples:
- Project manager Tom is getting used to that new air-conditioning system in the office.
- Jack's caddy car broke and he had to carry his clubs round the golf course. They were cumbersome at first but he's getting used to the weight of the bag now.

- Miss Humpington is getting used to the new air-conditioning system that they've set up in the stenographer's section.
- Doris is so used to wearing diamonds, she can't live without them!
- Matilda is getting used to having an empty space in her living room where the parrot cage once stood.

Exercise:

Student selects words from the box to fill in the blanks—sometimes they can appear more than once in the exercise examples. The first one has been done already to help you.

> air-conditioning system

a) On her first day in the office, Miss Happ couldn't understand why it was so cold or what the noisy whirring buzz in the corner window was. Distracted, she put things in the wrong files and called people by the wrong name. Now she's stopped making mistakes and doesn't need to complain to the maintenance department any more about the *air-conditioning system* in the office. You say: "Miss Happ's getting used to the *air-conditioning system* in her new job."

b) You are on your honeymoon in Venice with your wife. In the bridal gondola, you suddenly remember having forgotten to turn off the _____ back at the office and the consequent footprinty depletion of the planet's finite resources. You say: "Yes, the waves made the gondola roll a bit and it was strange at first. By the time we came off the lagoon it was the land that seemed weird! The _____ was still on back at the office."

c) Fedora hats used to be a very popular headwear, but (perhaps linked in some way to the advent, rise, and technical advancements of the _____) they have gone out of fashion. You say: "I wonder if fedoras went out of fashion because of _____?"

d) There used to be strikes. Not all workers were getting access to the _____ in office or home. Now the workers are getting used to new management policies and the market strategies of today—they think _____s are the biggest mistake since sliced bread.

e) Mr. Hash is not used to eating croque madames made with the wrong sort of cheeses! He says: "If they can't have the correct cheeses for a croque madame, then they could install a _____ in this restaurant—it's the least they could do."

f) You are explaining last quarter's sales figures to Dan Smith's marketing people when there's a knock at the door. You say (glancing at wristwatch): "Ah, that'll be the _____ now."

g) Having claimed to be on an important business trip, you sneak back into the office, with the intention of catching up on that filing backlog. In a specially adapted window you espy a neat slatted box device, neither in nor out of the room. You say: "No, I don't think I'll ever get used to these apparitions of Mr. Hash either—Oops! Look out! Someone's trying to defenestrate the _____."

See also commentary section on Social Convention below. Note that, in this connection, a habit can be seen as a mortally truncated eternal recurrence. Please note also that some of these examples are largely unhelpful. Discuss this with teacher.

31

Generally speaking, the "getting used to" form not only ferries us from the strangeness of a novel experience to the domesticated familiarity of the status quo, as Bob so helpfully points out, but it involves a principle of domesticating yin-yang reciprocity too. It is not merely a question of a subject getting used to *objects,* but a question of objects getting used to *subjects* in return. On that *Cat in the Hat* morning, for example, my having to familiarize myself with a new human eye, to chairs, doors, plastic spoons, the topography of the house, the positions of light switches, the ready mastery of bilabial fricatives, etc., was really only half the picture. For while things might have appeared strange to me, how strange *I* must have seemed to things around me. Tables, chairs, plastic spoons, light switches, throwing quizzical glances at one another, like a herd of stunned gazelles (imagine the hushed David Attenborough commentary) in the midst of whom an old boulder has been suddenly transformed into an affable lion. This tense form was a onetime darling of the turtlenecked, jazz-jiving, chain-smoking, bleak-mongering, rive-gauche, postwar, pre-head-butt existentialists—alas now extinct.

One of the beauties of the "getting used to" form is that it will apply to virtually any situation. It does not apply, however, to the following situation: tragically the milkman is trampled under a cow. His stand-in—the gentleman currently delivering milk to your doorstep for your morning bowl of

Cheerios—is your long lost identical twin. On the drive into work your car is overtaken by the electrical milk cart, driven by this long lost identical twin—and you find that you are tailing behind yourself. When you then arrive at your office, you find your twin is already there at your desk, screeching a nice big cheery *Morning, Mr. Hash!* like some kind of parrot. For the rest of that day, long lost identical twin proceeds to follow you about the office, mimicking your every gesture, repeating everything you say. Hungry or not, he shadows you to the canteen at lunchtime, decides *he* must have a *Belmont Gazette* too when you set off to the newsstand—and in any case, most vexing of all, proceeds to read your copy over your shoulder. On the first day this happens, his behavior is a trifle exasperating, to say the least. But when he turns up the next day and the day after that, things with the long lost identical twin only get worse. You cannot and do not get used to *those* sorts of apparitions.

Please note how there exists an elegant, refreshingly Edwardian variation of "used to" and that is "would do," as in, say, *"When the shops opened, the citizenry would dance in the streets and throw flowers on the keepers"*—a more literary form, imbued perhaps with a sense of melancholia, a tinged nostalgia for "times gone by" not found in the more matter-of-fact "used to." The technical term for this form is the past indicative. Do not confuse the past indicative with the conditional form—for example, *"If the shops opened, the citizenry would dance in the . . ."* Note also how the past indicative "would do" form cannot be applied to the verb "to be." We do not say "I would be" (in the sense of "I was"), but rather "I used to be," or more simply "I was." In the case of enduring habits, when the thing we used to do is something we still in fact do, we do not use the "used to" form when referring to the nascent stages of our habit—since this would imply we have given up the habit in question. Please note also how the past indicative form will sooner or later wither away and is therefore not worth learning.

32

Canard du Jour . . .
Écoutez et Répétez!

You and your briefcase are in a swanky rive-gauche restaurant in Paris, decorated in Third Republic fin de siècle style, with gilded bell-less mirrors on the walls. From your upstairs candlelit table there are window views of an eminently perchable Eiffel Tower and argonautless bateaux mouches plying to and fro on the river Seine. The strains of a romantic accordion can be heard playing at the bookstalls, locked up for the night on the quayside *trottoirs*.

For this exercise a small, well-thumbed pocket-size dictionary with phonetic spellings and soup stains has been placed at your disposal.

Having established, *malheureusement,* that oversize portions of hamburger and fries do not appear on this evening's menu, you have asked the waitress (in an abysmal hee-haw accent) for what you hope to be something close to traditional beans on toast. If all has gone well, the waitress will now bring you—

a) Rôti de petit lapin à la moutarde, or
b) Foie gras chaud poêlé aux blancs de poireaux, or
c) Canard Flaubertien à la rouennaise, or
d) Col de perroquet farci accompagné de mange-tout "à la façon de Mme. Hash," or
e) Croque madame accompagné des haricots blancs à la charentaise

While waiting for the waitress to bring the order, the student should pair the remaining menu items with the appropriate translation listed below on the napkin:

Stuffed parrot neck with Mrs. Hash–style beans/roast baby rabbit in mustard sauce/duck in nice dreamy sauce/fried duck liver with leeks in a sherry sauce.

The correct request for beans on toast should of course have been item *e*—the croque madame avec haricots blancs à la charentaise. Unfortunately, the waitress seems to have brought you what looks more like a fromage de tête with a side dish of cèpes à la sarladaise (brain cheese with edible boletus). In order to remedy the situation you should now say which of the following:

• Je ne croyais pas que j'avais commandé un potage de cerveau, *ou*
• Vous n'avez certainement pas écouté comme il faut, *ou*
• Du fromage, donc, *ou*
• Yuck—take it away!, *ou*
• Est-ce qu'il faut que j'attende le croque madame—par hasard?

Having toyed with the fromage de tête with a silver fourchette, the student should now:

a) order another fromage de tête with a side dish of cèpes à la sarladaise *ou*

b)   ask the waitress if she would like to join you on the
      midnight bateau-mouche trip, *ou*

c)   demand a canard à la canardaise—compliments of
      the chef, *ou*

d)   leave the restaurant abruptly and seek out the
      nearest Le Fast Food, *ou*

e)   have the fromage de tête tactfully replaced with a
      croque madame

As you wait for your croque to come, ask for the sommelier's
wine list, from which after great deliberation and detailed
debate regarding vintners' soil husbandry, feet hygiene, the so-
cioeconomic impacts of methods of calibration of pH and su-
crose levels, etc. (all in French; exaggerated hee-haw accents
permitted—up to a point) . . . you decide to stick with your original order of a brown fizzy drink with bubbles and high sugar
content with which to wash down your madame.

When the croque arrives, you readily ascertain that it does
not quite meet your expectations of what a real croque madame
ought to taste like. Once more with the help of your handy
pocket-size phrase book, upbraid the waitress for bringing you
the deficient repast. Stress that the recipe for a genuine croque
should use processed cheddar and not Gruyère, and that the
egg (or "oeuf") should remain "à cheval." In addition, the chef
would do better to avoid sprinkling in fragments of coquille at
the scrambling forchette phase. Ask her to forward your com-
ments without further delay on to the house chef, Monsieur le
(petit) chef—a short Dijonian dwarf whose erect starched chef's
hat you have been watching pass back and forth at the serving
hatch with industrious frequency. Have her make him understand that while that kind of croque may be acceptable to the
indigenous gourmands, for the more discerning palate of the
passing tourist such fare will simply not be tolerated.

"Monsieur 'Ash, c'est (pas) moi!"

33

What a pity that the author of such a toothsome contribution on edible comestibles cannot be here to join us! What dainty dishes the cook, the author—the thief!—has left on our table. No, *garçon*—don't touch that napkin—let's keep a place set in case he manages to make it after all.

For the monocular, monochromic monolinguist, however, this latest offering heralds a less palatable, less digestible possibility altogether: that Bob might be about to extend the reach of his mischief beyond the realm of his own native language. Not long ago, I expressed a concern vis-à-vis the appropriate use of the sky, stating, not unreasonably, that it should remain the preserve of the naturally airborne—aware perhaps of the danger that exposure to foreign tongues might give Bob bright ideas about new playgrounds for discombobulatory prankage. (*"I'm off to Acapulco to brush up on my Spanish, back in the office on Monday."*) But really, to tell the truth, this was an idle concern. The fact was that Bob already *had* ample enough access to other languages as things were—without having to so much as leave the runway tarmac at Belmont International Airport.

Parallel to Bob's picture book world there exists, under the Acme Institute's dependable aegis, a range of parallel picture book universes, each corresponding to a different language, each more or less taking the same basic format as *Forward with English!,* each presided over by their own folklorish equivalent of Bob. (We might note in passing that only *Forward with English!* is presided over—in tandem—by a parrot.) Now, not only did Bob already have ample access to this *mutually exclusive* material (arranged in an inviting lamplit display case in the office foyer), but he was already able to commune with his real-life counterparts, who, for cost-cutting reasons, had been installed by Acme no farther afield than on Remington Drive. We've already met Señor Gonzalez from the Spanish version with his orange tree and hammock in the garden, located not as some might have thought in some well-watered suburb of Madrid but in fact just two doors down from Bob; we have alluded more than once to Signor Brambilla from the Italian version (coat over shoulders in traditional *disinvolto* manner, milk cart thwarting Ferrari in the driveway). And now here's Monsieur Lafayette in his Breton pullover and beret (baguette under an arm, and a string of onions draped over the handlebars of his bicycle) with his expert knowledge of recipes.

If Bob ever fancied importing the odd mangled foreign phrase into his own course, all he had to do was borrow one from the front desk and rip off. To flesh out some exotic detail or add a little "foreign color" to his examples, he could rip off—or parrot—one of the foreign course books. It was as easy as nipping over the fence to bring back a badly aimed Frisbee armed with notebook and pencil.

On the other hand, if Bob thought that by sneaking over the fence into the neighboring yards and plundering those Acmatic siblings to *Forward with English!* he'd be able to derail *this* editor in chief—then I'm afraid he has underestimated the use to which his mascot had been putting his own free time.

It is a well-known fact that when a parrot is left alone for some time, a talking device of an electronic nature should be left running in the room. To the parrot, a humble wireless set, a left-on TV, can provide an endless source of amusement—the devices proving not only great companions in themselves, but often proving instructive to the bird's education itself. Adhering to this fine tradition, the Hash household enjoyed a regular ebb and flow of freebie foreign-language learning audiocassettes via Bob's workplace (borrowed from that lamplit display cabinet in the foyer) and, in addition, it subscribed to a mail-order company (a subsidiary of Acme) from which it received audio novels, read out by voices that sounded suspiciously like members of the cast from *Forward with English!*

As she was usually the last to leave the house in the mornings when she set off for the shops, it usually fell to Matilda to slot a tape into the cassette deck and leave it switched on (continuous loop facility). It is in large part thanks to Matilda's thoughtfulness that I have thus far been able to defuse Bob's cheap literary peccadilloes when they appeared on the horizon; it is thanks again to Matilda that I will now be in a position to disentangle any polyglot miscegenation that Bob cares henceforth to peddle.

Let us now brace ourselves for an onslaught of this new breed of tamper!

34

Phone Exercise

*"**K**önnen Sie mir auf der Karte zeigen, wo meine Golf-schläger sind—machen Sie schnell!"* = *"Can you show me on a map where my golf clubs are very quickly?"*

Now you have to imagine that you're going on a golfing tour of the Scottish links, renowned for their rugged seacoast views and treacherous bunkers. At the airport in Belmont you check in your clubs and board a flight to Prestwick International. However, on arrival at Prestwick, you are told that your golfing equipment has been mistakenly directed to Hamburg.

Student is given use of the customer service desk at Prestwick and put through to the lost property desk at the Hamburg airport—the task being to explain the situation, in German, to the Hamburg luggage assistant, stressing that you have a seven thirty tee-off on Monday morning. At student's request, a Bakelite phone apparatus (with exterior mounted bells) may be supplied to enhance authenticity of the exercise.

Before picking up the phone, student might like to look over the following useful key words and phrases:

die Golfschläger = the golf club
der Golfball = the golf ball
das Fenster = the window
es ist ein Unfall passiert = an accident has happened
ich füsselte mit der mit Luft Stewardess = I played footsie
    with the air hostess
er kann sich gut in andere Leute einfühlen = he is good at
    putting himself in other people's shoes
(slang) Nur schwätzen kanste, da steckt nichts dahinter =
    all you do is blather on; there's nothing behind it
nachplappern = to parrot
Gott im Himmel = goodness to Betsy

Student should also bear in mind possible pitfall puns involving the word "link":

linkisch = clumsy
Augennach links = eyes to the left
and
weder links noch rechts schauen = not to let oneself be
    distracted

None of which has anything to do with golf courses along the rugged windswept coastal regions of Scotland.

Student now will be ready to pick up the receiver and translate into German the following inventory of his missing golfing equipment: a Bennington pouch golf bag with a soft-brushed matte black leather trunk; a set of Dunlop LoCo 450cc woods with titanium-reinforced graphite shafts; a hook- and slice-reducing good luck mascot Deacon Brodie "spoon" with a persimmon shaft and blackthorn head protected by a tartan sock; a full set of Wilson Deep Red irons (for green approaches and rough management); in the left-hand zipper pocket of the bag itself there will be half a dozen brand-new apostolic dimpled Precept D-Force guttie 392 octahedron-pattern golf balls with velocity-enhancing ionomer cover and patented in-built Bergsonian time-warp effect; in the right side pocket there will be a Footjoy stay-soft golfing glove with an advanced, long-lasting, performance-enhancing leather grip; in the central upper pocket (or sporran) an assortment of Brush T wood professional tees in a variety of handsome impressionist's pastels together with several impressively birdie-rich scorecards and a partially nibbled cuttlefish (*ein Tintenfisch*) belonging to your pet parrot.

As you come to the end of your flawlessly translated descriptions, Heinrich at the lost luggage desk in Hamburg happens to catch sight of an unidentified golf bag emerging through a flap and trundling along the rubberized conveyor belt in front of his desk. Hauling it off (clatter of lugged clubs heard on the other end of the phone line), Heinrich now launches into an itemized listing of the bag and its contents. Here, the student's task is to translate any phrases remaining in English into simultaneously rendered German:

> HEINRICH (dismantling conveyor-belt golf bag): Ach so, wir haben sie hier ein dubbin-waxed, vermilion-hued, Ping Hoofer with mesh sleeves containing a three-quarter set of torque reducing boron-shafted Billy Knights . . .

> YOU (interrupting Heinrich before he goes any further): Nein. Das ist nicht meine Golftasche!

> Undeterred, Heinrich appears to have espied another golf bag on the conveyor belt and has now brought it forth for a similarly delivered description. . . .

> HEINRICH: Ja, we have now ein Titliest polymer golf bag with a weatherproof travel cover, a full complement of

Fastrax clubs, a set of Slazenger XTC overrun golf balls with a 408 dimple two-piece solid core—

You: Nein, nein! DAS IST NICHT meine Golftasche!

A veritable parliament of golf bags seems by now to have mounted the conveyor belt and is circling magisterially and unclaimed in front of the luggage assistant. One golf bag after another is lugged off the belt and described to you over the phone in flawless German. Surely one of zeez [sic] golf bags will turn out to be yours!

HEINRICH: Here ist ein Titliest opal polymer-bolstered trunk containing a somewhat depleted set of Future steel shafts, flight wing pockets containing seventeen Top-Flite Infinity golf balls. In the tee slots seven unused Eco tees—

You: Nein, DAS IST NICHT meine Golftasche.

HEINRICH: Okay. We have here also a set of Mitsushiba T-Pro betas in an albino white Bunker Ping Professional—

You (doodling on golfing scorecard with a tiny pencil): Nein, DAS IST NICHT meine Golftasche!

HEINRICH (helpfully): Or what about this ladies' set of Ogio O-Zone pink-shafted brassies with fur-lined cosies and an ovule-rich pouch of marsupial Volvik Crystals and a packet of emergency tampons? (The image of the Ogio O-Zones and the pink-shafted brassies recalls to mind the gently molded morphology of an inland course with wooded glades, smooth mown fairways, where, of an idyllic summer's afternoon, the student was once invited to make up the numbers on a languorous two-ball ladies' foursome. Student stops doodling and with spare non-telephone hand starts practicing "air swings"—sending imaginary Volvik Crystals through wistful parabolas into the Prestwick airport concourse with his trusty invisible niblick.)

You: DAS IST NICHT meine Golftasche!

Heinrich: And here we have a Club-Pro Snoopy-Yellow Youth Hip-Pop golf bag for Inca hepcats containing a set of Ecstasy flight shafts and Day-Glo rotundities—

You (beside yourself, through phlegm-rich smoker's cough, rediscovering the buried fruits of your night-class beginner's German): Viefele kraz muss ich so sagen, DAS IST NICHT MEINE Golftasche!

Clearly your rusty dog's-breakfast night-class German has been stretched to its limits. However, as the next bag's description progresses, it seems your patience is about to be rewarded . . .

Heinrich: Okay, Herr Hash, we'll give it one last shot. . . . Ach. So, we have hier [sic] a Bennington pouch golf bag with a soft-brushed matte black leather trunk . . .

You: Ja?

Heinrich: . . . a set of Dunlop LoCo 450cc woods with titanium-reinforced graphite shafts; a hook- and slice-reducing good luck mascot Deacon Brodie "spoon" with a persimmon shaft and blackthorn head . . .

You (hopes rising): Ja?

Heinrich: . . . with a tartan sock for protection . . .

You: Ja, ja, das ist gut.

Heinrich: . . . a full set of Wilson Deep Red irons (green approaches, rough management) . . .

You (imagining your one-armed bandit practice shot chip over a short Brazilian landing strip of fairway and—with satisfying *kerplunk*—land straight into the hole: auditory hallucination of polite, rippling Open applause muted in benevolent verdancy): Ja. Das ist sehr gut!

HEINRICH: . . . in the left-hand zipper pocket of the bag itself there are half a dozen brand-new apostolic dimpled Precept D-Force guttie 392 octahedron-pattern golf balls with velocity-enhancing ionomer cover and patented inbuilt Bergsonian time-warp effect . . .

YOU (with great fluency, growing certain): Jawohl!

HEINRICH: . . . in the right side pocket I see a Footjoy stay-soft golfing glove with advanced, long-lasting, performance-enhancing leather grip . . .

YOU: Jawohl! Jawohl! Natürlich!

HEINRICH: . . . in the central upper pocket (or sporran) wir haben ein [sic] assortment of Brush T wood professional tees in a variety of handsome impressionist's pastels together with several impressively birdie-rich scorecards . . .

YOU (blushing modestly): Ja. (And after a short Teutonic pause) Und?

HEINRICH : Und?

But it seems Heinrich has come to the end of his on-the-spot inventory.

YOU (persisting): Aber, der ist nicht ein Tintenfisch?

After some more zipping sounds and rattling of golf clubs on the other end of the line, Heinrich regrets to inform you that there is none.

YOU : Ein kleine bissen Tintenfisch hast du finden nicht? Bist du sicher?

Heinrich assures you that this golf bag is devoid of the merest fragment of Tintenfisch.

YOU (spluttering, incandescent): DAS IST NICHT meine Golftasche!

Following this rather exasperating final exchange, thank Kirstie, the pretty Prestwick attendant, for the use of her apparatus. Kirstie, who has been following your phone plight, conveys to you the news that your Golftasche has meanwhile been traced aboard Flight DF 46, and is currently flying from Lima to Wellington, New Zealand, from where it will be duly forwarded (like an Olympic Flame) on to Prestwick via Sydney, Singapore, and Heathrow, thus circumnavigating the entire globe.

YOU (phlegmatically): Gott im Himmel!

Then, in a more conciliatory tone, you ask, "Können Sie mir auf der Karte zeigen wo meine Golfschläger sind, machen Sie schnell!" Kirstie nods her head with a world-weary expression, taps a rustling, unfolded map with a blind, carefree finger.

"The funny thing is that just a few days ago there was another gentleman—also called Mr. Hash, incidentally—who, item for item, was in an identical fix!"

35

My own participation in the noble pastime of golf in fact pre-
dates the regular nine-thirty tee-off slot on Saturday mornings that I have now inherited—along with his wife and full
range of credit cards—from amateur athlete and internationally renowned Mr. Comedy of Errors himself, Bob T. Hash III.
As aficionados of the sport will well know, there is a small
but immaculately trimmed nine-hole twin-round municipal golf course located on the outskirts of Belmont. In the Popular Hobbies and Pastimes section
of the seventh edition of *Forward with English!*, Comenius
can be seen there, politely perched on the putter head of an
Odyssey Flash—protruding from a soft pouch Tai-Ping golf
bag.

That nine-thirty tee-off slot (Sats.) I now share, as Bob once
did, with a regular trio of buddy colleagues: Chester Cash from
accounts, Larry Bickwick from research and development, and
swanky Hank Redford, arch retiree from the fourth edition,
thumbs in his suspenders, puffing on a cigar.

And what better place to put the finishing touches to a
business deal than Belmont municipal inland golf links! Few
places are better to bask in the quiet success of last month's
sales figures than under the intimacy of an open sky. Where
better to muse on a wide range of topical topics—global warming, the widespread abuse of syntax, the road to world

peace—not to mention certain burning questions of meta-physics and personal identity. (Though they did say if I didn't stop shouting "fore" when they were putting—I'd not get invited again.)

36

Customs and Mores: "Think Globally, Act Locally"

You are a management consultant on a business trip and have just arrived at the airport in Prague, Golden City of Spires, on a cold and foggy February morning. A taxi is now taking you from the airport to your hotel in the center of town and has just turned onto Wenceslas Square, where you observe a burly, mullet-headed gentleman permitting his dog to defecate with impunity upon the sidewalk. Though he is standing not five paces from a municipal poop-deposit bin, it is clear that the man has no intentions of removing the nervous little turd. You ask the taxi driver to execute an emergency halt and to put the meter on hold for the duration of this exercise.

Student's task: Getting to know the locals!
Wind down your taxi window and inform the indigenous sausage dog owner—in English—that his charge has just paid an unscheduled visit to the restroom. Explain to him how the offending stool can be scooped up and deposited in the appropriate poop bin, which you indicate without having to leave the comfort

of your taxi. At first, no concession should be given to the possi-
bility that the gentleman may not in fact speak English with na-
tive fluency. (LANGUAGE TIP! A raised, imperious voice may
work wonders in these kinds of situations.) Where the subject
proves less than cooperative, and till his English (not to mention
that of the taxi driver) improves, you may wish to make use of
some of your level three Czech. As you reenact the scenario
above, try to use as many of the following native Czech words
and phrases as you can. These you will find in the pocket phrase
book that the taxi driver, rabbit-from-hat style, has now pro-
duced from his glove compartment for his passenger's conve-
nience:

ahoj, nejde otevřít okno = ahoy, the window won't open
(as ice breaker) promiňte, může se zde parkovat? = excuse
    me, is it possible to park here?
ahoj, můžete mi zkontrolovat pneumatiky? = ahoy, can you
    check my tires?
ano, mluvím s tebou = yes, you, I am speaking to you
slavíte něco, můj starý okurkový kamaráde? = are you
    celebrating something, my old cucumber friend?
jste v Praze poprvé? = is this your first time in Prague?
promiňte, jak se dostanu na Hlavní nádraží = can you tell
    me how to get to the central station?
bohužel, tyto okurky mi (moc)nechutnají = I (don't) like
    the cucumber very much, unfortunately
(to bystander—that hot dog vendor, for example) prosím
    vás dosvěcíte mi to? = excuse me, can I call on you as a
    witness?
bez okurky, prosím = without cucumber, please
proč jsi to udělal = why did you do it?
já okurky nebudu= for me no cucumber, thank you
tento dřevěný panáček je dělaný ručně = is this wooden
    puppet made by hand?
jaký je vlastně nyní tvůj handicap v golfu = what is your
    golf handicap these days, by the way?

cítím se mizerně jako papoušek = I feel as sick as a parrot
ahoj, neměli byste něco proti nevolnosti? = ahoy, have you
   got something I could take for nausea?
myslím že, operní sezóna začne za dva týdny = I believe
   the opera season begins in a fortnight
lepši vrabec v hrsti, nežli holub na střeše = better an egg
   today than a hen tomorrow
příjemnóu cestu! = enjoy the rest of your stay!

Quoting the Latin adage *tempus volat,* advise the gentleman with the small incontinent dog that he should take up
English lessons perhaps sooner rather than later, thereby
avoiding this kind of unnecessary confusion in future. Explain
to him, moreover, that you are an affiliated member of the animal liberation front and that you believe it is cruel to make a
dog wear a muzzle.

Now tell the taxi driver to reactivate his meter and proceed to the
requested destination!

Bringing up Directions again at this stage is a good way perhaps to check on our bearings, and serves as a way of testing both the student's retention capacities as well as the general effectiveness of the Acme customized manual's methodology. I am now in the happy position to declare that the forthcoming eighth edition of *Forward with English!* will be safe for general consumption.

Notice how the tow-haired, goatee-bearded, atelier-dwelling picture book artist has used none other than Bob as the model for the "management consultant" in question, his pocket stuffed with a taxidermist's fat-cat wad of 200 Kc banknotes. In an early draft sketch (which I happened to find among his notes), Bob and the artist have the visitor (dashing jawline, bowler hat, decidedly undisorientated visage) shouting out from his taxi window if the man with the dog could tell him the way to Big Ben—and getting cross when he couldn't. In my own upholstered version, that famous clock tower has been converted to the Astronomical Clock in Old Town Square with its parade of apostles. I use a well-loved parable from Kafka wherein a bland and hapless tourist (knapsack, plus fours, jackdaw, and a four-knotted hankie) respectfully requests directions to the castle. I do not use the dog prop. I do not involve taxis and I do not truck with turds. The castle's jagged, serrated spires loom over the city and the gentle dogleg bend in the river. . . . *"No, sir, I said tourists are not permitted to jump out that window."*

Social Conversations:
Some Useful Small Talk

At the office party you find yourself cornered at the drinks
table by Tushi Moto. Now onto his second glass of corpo-
rate punch, Tushi is keen to practice his English by discussing
market strategies and to tell you about last weekend's "sub-
liminal sales training workshop for rapid market penetration,"
which, due to unforeseen circumstances, you were unfortunately unable to attend in person. Here are some of the things
Tushi might say to you and some excuses you might think of
using to make your getaway and resume your tête-à-tête with
Miss Green over at the photocopier. The excuses are of varying
levels of tact: see which is your personal favorite!

> Tushi Moto: Hi, Jack! Say, those new flip charts sure are
> a great improvement on the old ones.

> You (refilling glasses in haste): Excuse me a sec. Miss
> Green seems to be having some difficulties with the pho-
> tocopier. I'd better go and see if she needs my expert as-
> sistance . . .

TUSHI MOTO: Great party! They sure know how to lay out a good spread for the employees round here.

YOU (glancing theatrically at wristwatch with big exaggerated looking-at-wristwatch type gestures): That's right, Tushi. Sorry, can't hang around, that cloud looks like rain!

TUSHI MOTO: Our market share has improved, Jack—but I still say there's always room for further improvement.

YOU (wineglass in either hand, one for you, the other for Miss Green, elbowing Tushi aside with office bonhomie): Excuse me while I fetch myself a drink.

TUSHI MOTO: Hi, Jack. Have you seen the latest sales report yet? Sales are up again, third quarter in a row. The way I see it, Jack, our trained sales force is the best!

YOU (author of said report, yawning loudly): I'm afraid the dog chewed mine to bits the other night. See you at the marketing convention. . . .

TUSHI MOTO: At the training seminar they told us if you want to clinch that important sale, your ideal customer is the kind of person who looks over the fence into their neighbor's garden and goes, "Hey, see that jet-stream hi-tech turbo-boost Bach monsoon carpet-splash sprinkler? I WANT one of those too!"

YOU (gesturing wildly toward party dips in the background): Sorry, Tushi, gotta run. Grandma's not been up to snuff these days. . . .

TUSHI MOTO: . . . and they were saying how the key to a successful, carefree lifestyle is to avoid words like "problem." . . . Keep the tone upbeat and focus on the thing you want to sell. . . . The key phrase (if, say, you're trying to sell sprinklers, for example) is "You look as if you're ready to own one of our monsoon mimic garden sprinklers."

YOU (pointing dramatically out window, mock staggering backward and away from the probable trajectory of a falling quince): Crikey, Tushi, there's a quince on that roof! Look out behind you. I think it's going to roll off! (*Student crouches, nips off toward the photocopying area. Tushi in confusion.*)

TUSHI MOTO: I like to unwind in front of the television in the evenings.

YOU (a purdeaf [sic] botanist's brow): I wonder if that spider plant by the photocopier is a real one or plastic? I must go and check . . .

Tushi's voice tailing off behind you as you speed over toward Miss Green. Student might think of these expressions as adaptable templates where key words and phrases can be substituted to suit a variety of circumstances. It is worth learning a few excuses by heart—you never know when you might need them!

You got the right upbeat attitude there, Jack! You sure you didn't sneak into the workshop last weekend when no one was looking?

39

Unfortunately for some of us, there can be no excuses for coming up with *that* sort of unhelpful exercise, with its trumped-up apprehensions on behalf of the quince, with its side-glancing sneer at training workshops, and its unwarranted employment of fast-track stereotypes.

On the other hand, it is perhaps fitting that the matter of office parties should come up at this stage—given the current infectious atmosphere of excitement now surrounding the announcement, next Friday, of last quarter's sales figures. The signs, as always, are in evidence, with boxes of fizzy wine and a choice of jamboree dips appearing in the office kitchenette, and cartons of streamers and inflatable balloons stacked up beside the photocopier. (This quarter, one box has already been opened ahead of schedule.) How easy to get swept along by the buzz of excitement among staff, how easy to get distracted from one's more sober literary endeavors, should one have such things. How easy to lose sight of a by-now-emerging threat to my position—a very great threat indeed.

As we can see, my little excursion as Bob T. Hash III's stand-in seems so far to have been going very smoothly. If anything, things have been going a little *too* smoothly to be true—the coincidences falling just a little too generously, statistically speaking, in my favor: the effortless slipping into Bob's shoes, the blossoming romance with his wife, Mr. Gleason's happy acceptance of any (often quite drastic) reparative alterations made to the errant *Forward with English!*

That's not to say I've not now and again wondered about what might have become of Bob after his secret rendezvous at the airport—picturing him and his russet consort against a variety of multiplex Dolby-sound wide-screen refugee backdrops. Apart from that poolside bamboo umbrella in Acapulco, I've imagined them cruising through red baked canyons at sunset in an open-topped fifties sedan. I've pictured a bemused, dune-crossing, camel-mounted Lawrence in the Maghreb, a be-veiled concubine Scarlett on the camel tethered to the rear; I've imagined them sipping champagne in an elegant dining car of a Trans-Argentinian rail wagon on a vast forgotten pampa; I've imagined them wrapped up in thick white pile towels at health spas. I've pictured them on some low-season cruise to the antipodes, leaning over the deck rail to admire cute little penguins diving off a starboard-side ice floe into the sea.

Yet however geographically distant or exotically removed from Belmont I might have imagined them to be, I've not been able to quite shake off a sneaking sense that the dastardly duo are perhaps far less distant than I would like. In fact I've never quite been able to get rid of an ominous feeling that somebody has been, as it were, reading over my shoulder. And the further my worthy labor of de-obfuscation progresses, the more certain I'm becoming that I'm being shadowed, that my own moves are sometimes actually being *anticipated* by somebody else.

And it does not take a Pulitzer Prize for grammatical phrase books to work out who that someone might be.

40

Gondola Skit:
"Come in, Number Cinque!"—
a chance to practice your Italian!

Y̲ou and your wife are honeymooning in Venice. One late afternoon—after a somewhat extended siesta—you decide to hire a gondola for a trip on the canals. The skit begins toward the end of your voyage, with your rental time running out and the gondolier (a certain Ragioniere Brambilla) attempting to pilot the sleek craft back to its moorings. It so happens that Ragioniere Brambilla's favorite association football team has an important match that will be broadcast live on television this evening. Since he is keen to watch it, he wishes to berth his vessel and retire for the evening with a somewhat uncharacteristic degree of promptitude. The game begins in less than an hour.

Note to language instructor: familiarize students with the basic situation above before having them act out the following possible complications that might develop. A list of words and phrases the student may find useful can be found below.

a) Tell the gondolier that you don't want to go ashore yet. Ask him to take you out into the lagoon so that you and your wife can lie back on the cushions and watch the sunset—after all, it is your honeymoon!

b) Tell the gondolier that you will drop him ashore and take the helm yourselves, promising to return his gondola safely to the quay when you've finished with it.

c) Tell the gondolier that returning so abruptly to shore is making your wife feel seasick. Ask him to divert his course to the nearest pharmaceutical outlet.

d) An insistent gull has landed on the prow and is spoiling your view. Ask the gondolier to kindly remove it.

e) The gondolier's mother phones him on his cell phone to tell him that his spaghetti is on the table and that if he doesn't hurry up he will be late for the kickoff.

f) The gondolier's mother has now appeared in person on the hump of an old bridge with a bag of freshly laundered clothes. Tell the gondolier to ignore her and to speed up his punting.

g) Your gondola has just had a minor collision with a hearse-boat carrying a shiny black coffin (the deceased having fallen to his death by falling from a window). You must now wait for the carabinieri to come and take a statement of maritime mishap.

h) You are the gondolier. Tell the passengers that you think a leak has sprung in your boat and that you've forgotten to bring life jackets. . . .

Some useful words and phrases. The translation is given in each case to help you:

nullis amor est sanabilis herbis = there is no herb to cure us of love (Ovid, *Metamorphoses*)

ho paura degli squali nella laguna = I'm afraid of the
    lagoon sharks

semel in anno licet insanire = once a year it's okay to go
    crazy

terra sis illi laevis/fuit illa tibi = earth, lie as light on her
    as she trod on you . . . (Ovid)

ho sentito che la partita sará rimandata à causa di un
    piccolo incidente inaspettato = I'm told that the match
    has been unexpectedly postponed

per fortuna trasmettono su Canale 5 i punti salienti dopo
    il telegiornale = luckily you'll get the highlights on
    channel 5 after the news

tu quoque, Brute, filii mihi? = you cook, my brutal files?

psittacus mortus est. Psittacus novus die vivat! = the
    parrot is dead. Long live the parrot!

And don't forget:

Un cetriolo va affettato con cura, condito con pepe ed aceto,
ed infine buttato via, come buono a niente. (Dr. Johnson's famous comment on cucumbers, from *Journal of a "Trip" to the
Hebrides.*)

41

Trust a thoughtless, birdbrained amateur like Bob T. Hash III to put that crass-beaked scavenger on the gondola prow (scenario *d*). In *my* version, the gull has been banished to some godforsaken landfill; while the honeymooners now proffer nutty tidbits to a lovable parrot.

As part of my own invaluable fieldwork research for this exercise, I took my wife for a spin round Duck Pond on a hired rowboat ($3.50/hr.). It may be true, to Duck Pond there is little of Canaletto or Turner—no golden church domes or ancient peeling palace façades on the shore. But the views of the golf course and, on that particular evening, a quite spectacular Venus were not to be sniffed at either. There was the timeless sensation of bobbing on water. You will see that in my version I have been able not only to eradicate Bob's nautical errors and footballing faux pas but to recapture some of the appropriate spirit of romance.

"Twenty-two degrees centigrade," said Matilda, on our little research trip, wetting her finger and sticking its glistening Lady Macbethian pinkness above her head, "with a light two knot south-westerly . . ."

"Darling, have I told you about this quarter's sales figures?" I said.

"They are dramatic. You told me about them at breakfast." As she said this, Matilda fluttered her eyebrows and did a three-quarter turn of the oar blade.

"It's becoming clear: someone has been tampering with the sales figures after all. . . . You know, I've been thinking again about our honeymoon in Venice. It was the most aqueous, Venice-like honeymoon I've ever been on."

"That makes two of us."

"I'm afraid it might actually make three. Did you not notice how that red-clad dwarf kept popping up on the canal walks— look out, there's a quince—No, hang on, look out, we're going to get stuck in those reeds on the shore—Here, let me punt!"

And indeed, the vessel's prow had nosed its way inadvertently into a floating temple of lilies. With our hire time running out, we appeared to have become enlodged in the crepuscular bower of a weeping willow, an oar floating off into a new example for the Everyday Accidents and Domestic Mishaps page. Thick velvet cushions lay in abundance on the leakproof planks of the hull. . . .

Gosh, all this work is making me hungry again!

42

An Invitation to Dinner

Mr. Brambilla is on a business trip to Prague. After a busy day finalizing the terms of a contract, he and his wife, who has accompanied him on the trip, have been invited by Pan Novák, his Czech associate, to the Nováks' apartment for an evening of dinner, relaxation, and cultural exchange.

The Brambillas, having showered and changed for the evening back at their central hotel, now find themselves dropped off by taxi (the cattleyas at Mrs. Brambilla's decollation having suffered a dislodgement, involuntary or otherwise) at a modest block of apartments located in a quiet outer suburb of the city. But apart from a small dog (presumably a long-haired dachshund) yelping behind a neighbor's door on the communal landing (set off by Mrs. Brambilla's clattering heels), the block of apartments would appear to be eerily uninhabited. It is something of a surprise, then, when a door opens to reveal a period hat stand, a shoe rack, and the hospitable Nováks.

The two business associates shake hands warmly and introduce their wives in the vicinity of the shoe rack. (Note to

student: playing the role of *Mr. Brambilla, apologize, in Czech,
for being a little late. Explain how the traffic/taxi driver/
hotel administration is to blame.*) Mrs. Brambilla presents Paní
Nováková with a packet of gift-wrapped pasta and a jar of
Genovese pesto, which are placed on a little table to the side of
the shoe rack. (*Now take the role of Mrs. Novák: express gratitude for the presents in Italian.*) Introductions over and gifts
presented, the Brambillas naturally expect to move out of the
narrow windowless hallway and forward into the body of the
flat but at the same time are conscious of a certain reluctance
to do so on the part of their hosts, who remain pointedly within
the orbit of the shoe rack. Mr. Novák now explains how in
Czechoslovakia it is customary for people coming indoors to remove their shoes at the threshold, where they exchange them
for a pair of interior carpet slippers, depositing the street shoes
on the shoe rack, where they can be readily identified and thus
retrieved on departure, on surrender of the slippers. This ap-
plies particularly to residents and, while not so rigorously ap-
plicable to visitors, is available to them if they so wish to follow
the system and for whom these nice pairs of interior and soft
African gray carpet slippers of various sizes are at their ready
disposal. (*You are Mr. Brambilla. Explain—from now on in
English—to the Nováks that while in Italy there does exist a
penchant for flip-flops on floor tile, your wife will not take kindly
to being seen in the ugly footwear currently on offer. You might
like to remind your hosts that you have already brought them
a present—hinting at possible further bribes if the ritual be
waived.*)

　　The be-slippered Brambillas have now moved through into
the Nováks' living room, where they sit on the settee nursing
small glasses of Becherovka. Mrs. Novák is passing round a
tray of pickled gherkins (*okurky*) and cucumber (*okurek*) with a
variety of lard-rich mayonnaise dips. (*You are Mrs. Brambilla:
compliment your hostess on the deliciousness of the gherkins.
Ask your hostess for the recipe for the dips.*)

By the third glass of Becherovka and round of gherkins our guests are beginning to wonder when dinner will be served. Since their arrival, except to replenish the tray with gherkins and dips, Mrs. Novák has not been through to the kitchen to check on anything that might be roasting in the oven, or to stir something that might be simmering on the stove. In fact the only signs of dinner so far are a bowl of coleslaw sitting on a kitchen counter visible from the settee, and a faint, rather distant smell of something piscine.

Just as the Brambillas begin to entertain the possibility that the gherkins and cucumber dip tray are meant to be dinner, they hear a strange splashing sound presumably from a bathroom. (*As Mr. Novák, explain that somebody, such as their delightful daughter in the mantelpiece photo, is not taking a bath.*) The party is invited to come through into the tiny narrow bathroom to investigate the source of the splashing noise.

It should be said that Mrs. Brambilla is no stranger to horror movies—there is nothing she likes so much as to thigh-clamp an armrest and gasp at a monster crawling out of the depths. Yet little could quite have prepared her for the sight of the boorish, humorless pond carp treading the murk against an imaginary current of mud in the Nováks' half-filled little bath. (*As Mrs. Novák, reassure your guests that, so long as they don't put their hands into the water, the carp will not bite them.*)

Suddenly Mr. Novák, glowing with pride, announces he will go fetch the *kladivo*. The Brambillas, remaining squeezed into the tiny bathroom with their hostess and of course having no idea what a *kladivo* might be, make polite conversation by asking her if her pet carp has a name and then ask her what is a *kladivo*. Mrs. Novák tells her guests that the carp is nameless and apologizes that she doesn't know the word for *kladivo* either in Italian or English, but says they'll soon see one for themselves. She then asks her guests if they would like to keep the "duše" to take back for their children in Italy. (CULTURAL TIP! The duše is the fleshy air sack gland inside the head of the carp, located, apparently, to the rear of the brain. In many ways a forerunner to the executive stress toy, the duše is cherished by Bohemian children as the soul of the carp.)

While the condemned dinner spends its final earthly moments mooning about in the murky bath, obliviously dreaming of its pond far from the maddening limelight and waggling its shoelacelike tentacle things, there comes from some cupboard in the Nováks' apartment the sound of someone rifling through a metal toolbox. (As Mrs. Novák, translate into Italian for your guests your husband's shouted question: "Where did you put that carp hammer, darling?") Mrs. Novák shouts back that it is probably under the sink in the kitchen where he left it. With culinary pride she informs her guests that in a few moments the carp will be served with a side dish of larded dumplings.

Presently, Mr. Novák, brandishing the "kladivo na kapra," returns to the bathroom. On his reappearance, as if sensing a great and imminent danger, the carp executes a sudden hairpin turn at the tap end of the bath, rounding it off with a violent tail thrash that splashes the hem of Mrs. Brambilla's evening dress with droplets of the foul-smelling water. Taking little heed to the distress this has caused his guest, Mr. Novák now kneels down at the shore of the bath and begins rolling up his cardigan sleeves. . . .

Some useful Czech phrases:

bez okurky, prosím = without pickled gherkins (*Am. Eng.:* *"pickles"*), please
zouvat se = remove one's shoes
botník = shoe rack
bačkory = slipper, backers
ten kapr nekouše = the carp doesn't bite
ještě jednou okurky, prosím = another helping of pickled gherkins, please
kladivo = hammer

Ahoj, kam jsi dal to kladivo na kapra, miláčku? = Where
did you put that carp hammer darling?

You might also like to inquire of the Nováks where they per-
formed their daily ablutions in the days leading up to the
slaughter. Discuss in class.

*Finally, as Mrs. Brambilla, suggest it is time to put on the water
for pasta—"De Cecco, Farfalle (93), pasta di semola di grano
duro; cottura 12 min, 10 al dente."*

43

If only Bob could have brought to his leavings the sane, sober, professional tone—in short, the sheer gravitas—that his endorsed successor would later bequeath to the scene!

The problem I'd like to highlight here, in Bob's version—leaving aside for a moment the grammatical tomfoolery and the shameless ransacking of foreign tongues—is a question of factual verisimilitude, or rather a lack thereof, a tendency toward the factual al dente, if you will, on the part of my mentor. Where I will boldly go "into the field" (that row round Duck Pond), Bob is simply too often unwilling or—more accurately—quite simply too *lazy* to carry out anything beyond the most perfunctory research. The factual discrepancies found in the carp exercise are symptomatic of a more general attitude of sloppiness toward anthropological matters throughout. That warren of cobbled, betaverned backstreets, the old wooden waterwheel revolving slowly into the night with droplets of water cascading from the blades (catching silver pearlets of Bohemian moonlight), the yellow monkish glow from a solitary scholar's window at the monastery library at Strahov—all *that* of course rings true. But now look closer at the foliage on the lindens: lime-green, sap-rich—existent!—thereby inverting the earth's magnetic poles to transplant a charming *mitteleuropean* yuletide tradition right plonk in the middle of summer, when in all likelihood the Nováks would have scurried off to their country cottage to brew up the samovar under the cherry tree, gorging themselves not on carp but on cucumbers and lard.

If Bob had actually taken the trouble to set foot in Prague (as opposed to throwing his Frisbee into the Nováks' garden around meal time and sneaking up to their dining room window with his notepad), he would know how (notwithstanding centuries of its laying concerted siege to the Czechoslovakian larder) the gherkin has still to be introduced to those faraway shores. He would know also that the miniature leviathan meets its end not by means of the bloody bludgeoning, to the brink of which the above ichthyophagous scenario brings us (no doubt potentially injurious to the bathtub itself), but with a straightforward tug on the plug chain.

We remember, in addition, how parrots exist uniquely in *Forward with English!* Out of no doubt noble intentions, Bob and the picture book artist had installed in the above a genetically modified toucan, placing it in a cozy corner of the Nováks' residence. Noble but mistaken—for the genetically modified toucan has a reprehensibly cavalier attitude to the intricate usage of the Czech system of cases, a failing that could easily sow confusion in the tender, impressionable ears of lady learners especially. Said interloper (the cheek!) has now been airbrushed out of the above, and released into the vast arboreal greenhouse of the local botanical gardens in Belmont. Its removal in no way diminishes the overall didactic value of the exercise.

Please note also how in my own final version of this section I have added strategically placed bowls of unsalted peanuts to go with the aperitifs. All references to carp have been removed.

44

Comprehension Test

Read over the story so far and then answer these questions. On the answer sheet, mark the letter corresponding to your choice (the answer key will be found at the back of the book). The first question has been done for you:

1. Señor Gonzalez went to the airport because
   a) the airport was handy
   b) he was going on an important business trip
   c) it was an unscheduled flight
   d) the seat belt sign came on during takeoff
   e) he did not go to the airport

The correct answer is *b*. He was going on an important business trip.

2. Bert was at the newsstand in the Alpine resort because
   a) Bert liked mountains and lakes
   b) the *Belmont Gazette* was on sale there
   c) he was on vacational employment

    d) he was ubiquitous

    e) he knew the route to the hotel

3. Miss Scarlett is late for work because
   a) she has been caught in a traffic jam
   b) she has been abducted by space aliens
   c) she is stuck in the elevator
   d) she has had a skiing accident
   e) she doesn't arrive in the office till nine fifteen

4. Construction engineer Jack suggests Bob take up
   Swahili lessons because
   a) it will look good on Bob's resume
   b) Jack is Swahili
   c) Bob is Swahili
   d) Bob has money to burn; Jack gets an (undisclosed)
      commission
   e) it is always a good idea to take advantage of a
      special offer!

5. The new edition of the *Forward with English!* course
   book has so far failed to appear in the shops because
   a) the shop manager has decided not to stock it
   b) nobody really wants to learn English these days
   c) the current edition has been such a great success
   d) the new course book is in the shops after all
   e) Mr. Gleason, the printer's assistant, has put
      things on hold till some last-minute amendments
      arrive

6. I'M A GREAT GUY got promoted because
   a) he deserved it
   b) the company was expanding its facilities
   c) he was responsible for launching the new socially
      responsible package for the valet overnight suit
      press we agreed on at the workshop
   d) Dr. Horowitz had messed up on the dosage
   e) he likes to get promoted

7. Cattleyas underwent an (involuntary) decollation in the taxi because
   a) they were late for the meeting and the carp was getting impatient
   b) it was taxicab regulations regarding that species of flower
   c) Signora Brambilla sneezed with a measure of violence
   d) Bob Hash's hand slipped again
   e) it sounded like a good idea at the time

8. The police are still conducting their inquiries because
   a) the tax forms haven't been completed properly
   b) the police like conducting extended inquiries
   c) the inquiries fell out the window
   d) the suspect has not yet been apprehended
   e) the police are not aware of any misconduct

45

Bob would certainly *like* to think that it was merely the police's inquiries that were discharged from that window. It is in any case customary (*see below,* Anything to Declare?) to dispose of unwanted documents by other, more environmentally friendly means (shredders, burning, teething dogs). The rate of acceleration of a body falling to earth is 9.81m/s^2. The sensitive learner will appreciate a certain tragic irony in this choice of example.

46

"Anything to Declare?"
a role play at customs and excise

Now you have to imagine that you are employed as a customs official at the busy terminal at Belmont International Airport. The scene is set with passengers lining up at flight gates, pilots and stewardesses striding purposefully across the main concourse. In the baggage area a vaguely familiar set of jet-lagged golf clubs on the carousel conveyor belt goes round and round in an unclaimed cameo.

Students act out the following scenarios, in each of which the accused, after extensive interrogation, turns out in fact to be entirely innocent of the charge. Once through, switch student roles and repeat. To make things more "realistic," the language instructor might like to procure a peaked cap for the customs official, and play the airport background ambience cassette (echoing heels in the concourse, velveteen flight announcements over the PA system) during role plays. (CULTURE TIP! The more certain the customs official of his/her intuition, and the more indignant the holidaymaker(s), the more entertaining this exercise tends to be.)

- Two suntanned Olympian ladies' doubles volleyball play-ers on flight 243 to Acapulco are attempting to pass through the nothing-to-declare exit. The customs de-partment has received advanced information that one or other—or both—of the volleyball players have concealed about their persons a small but valuable quantity of high-grade ergotine. In the interests of modesty the in-terview has been adjourned to a side room with nice comfy matrimonial-style cushions. Begin skit with the volleyball players down to lycra shorts and matching bikini tops (in team colors), with the customs official sat-isfied that the illegal substance is not to be found in their personal effects. . . .

- A notorious smuggler of contraband turbo-monsoon garden irrigation industrial sprinklers is apparently at large, planning the most audacious project of his career—to flood the fledgling Scottish market with an unprecedented quantity of the sprinklers, which appar-ently are being smuggled through in golf bags. . . .

- You have received a reliable tip-off that Belmont Inter-national Airport is being used as an exchange point by a ring of unscrupulous parrot smugglers. As chief customs official, your suspicions have in this connection been aroused by a passenger wearing a Bermuda shirt and a straw hat who, besides being rather overearnest in the exchange of the preliminary pleasantries, appears to be in possession of a talking suitcase with an uncannily parrotlike voice. Suspecting this to be a suitcase full of hallucinating parrots, you have the suitcase opened. On subsequent interrogation of one of its occupants, you discover that the parrot is under the illusion that it has

turned into a human being—having usurped its erstwhile mentor and thwarted a dastardly scheme to flood
the world with an apocryphal grammar primer. . . .

*LANGUAGE TIP! Where possible try to avoid the use of
foreign words and phrases to pad over gaps in your vocabulary.
"Scrambling"—or gratuitous (and often wildly disconnected)
polyglotism—should also be discouraged.*

At the foot of page 5 of the morning edition of last Thursday's *Belmont Gazette,* there was a small article indicating the disappearance of a certain Miss Scarlett, native citizen of Belmont and model employee at the Acme International Institute of Languages. According to friends and colleagues interviewed by that illustrious tabloid, in the run-up to her disappearance Miss Scarlett had shown no sign whatsoever of the slightest disaffection, psychological imbalance, or Rilkian wanderlust. On the evening before her presumed disappearance she and a colleague had eaten a pizza at Mario's on Main Street and she had packed a suitcase for a ski trip. Her apartment was tidy, her office files were in order. Belmont is a law-abiding city. While a perfunctory dredging of the pure-flowing River Caxton had been conducted, and a pack of sniffer hound dogs had (twice) been sent round the local nine-hole golf course, the impression given by the article was that the police had carried these things out more as some kind of practice drill than as any concern for a threat to Miss Scarlett's actual welfare. The general tone was no more tragic than if the article had been reporting that Miss Scarlett had gone off on a week's skiing trip to the mountains, which as it would later turn out, she had!

No mention was made at any point in the article of a missing Bob T. Hash III; and no appeal was made for information leading to his whereabouts.

Guess Who I Saw . . . ?

G uess who I saw down on the beach promenade, slinking away from a pile of garments discarded above an outgoing tide?"

"Bob T. Hash III?"

Bob T. Hash III is correct! Now see if you can answer the following questions with equal alacrity and aplomb. In each case, choose from the list of given possibilities (answers to be found at the back of the book):

a) Guess who I saw milling around at the mall yesterday morning, a battered leather briefcase under his arm, breakfasting on a takeout doughnut? (Warren Crosby/ Chester Cash/Jack the construction engineer/a security guard/Bob T. Hash III)

b) Guess who I saw peeking from behind the curtains of the lodgings in Bellville? (the dwarf chef from the French restaurant/Lucinda the Ping-Pong player/Señora

Gonzalez/the editor of the *Belmont Gazette*/Bob T. Hash III)

c) Guess who I saw making his getaway in a golf buggy in some farcical slow-motion car chase? (Mr. Gleason the printer's assistant/Heinrich from Hamburg/Christopher Columbus/Lee Trevino/Bob T. Hash III)

d) Guess who I saw taking a siesta in Señor Gonzalez's garden hammock? (Señor Gonzalez/Gulliver the Grammarian/Steve Winshaw/Señora Gonzalez/Bob T. Hash III)

e) Guess who I saw perched on a patch-eye pirate's shoulder? (Dr. Horowitz/Miss Novák/the wise owl on the way to Bellville/the patch-eye pirate's identical twin/Bob T. Hash III)

f) Guess who I saw trying to turn back the clock hands when no one was looking? (Winfield Norton/Miss Ratcliffe/the Cat in the Hat/the horologist/Bob T. Hash III)

g) Guess who came to clean out the birdcage and remove the cuttlebone from the bars of the cage in the process? (Dan Arbuckle/Mick Aldehyde/Miss Scarlett/Factotum Bert/Bob T. Hash III)

h) Guess who popped up in the office foyer the other day and started interrogating the concierge about the upcoming office party? (Signora Brambilla/The concierge's long-lost identical twin/the olive-skinned, almond-eyed, trilingual jet-black ponytailed receptionist from the Hotel Bristol/Bob T. Hash III)

"I doubt it, Thomas. Didn't you hear Bob had a tragic accident at the office? You probably saw somebody who just looks like him."

49

The first tangible evidence that someone might be taking an unwelcome interest in my repair work on the new *Forward with English!* came in the form of an apparently anonymous memo, delivered to my in tray just a few days after I'd made my first test submission to the printers. Composed largely in the tone of a routine pronouncement and distributed not only to my own illustrious in tray but to those of all desks on my floor and to all floors underneath (Fifth floor's the highest she goes, madam), the memo began with an outline of the new fire drill procedure before suddenly rounding off with a warning to employees to be on the lookout for what it called "oddity of linguistic intrusion"—a rather cryptic formulation in itself, one might note, and, to my eyes, a distinct giveaway as to its authorship. No indication was given where said intrusions might become manifest (in grammatical tips announced over the public-address system?), nor as to their possible source (from within the husbandry of the tenses itself?); nor was there any suggestion as to what action should be taken if any such intrusions were encountered.

Needless to say, someone was being nosy, and, despite the banality of its terms and the vagueness of its object, I did not regard this memo development in a particularly favonian light. That morning, I had to force myself to join in the office canteen chortle, pretend to agree with the general opinion of my colleagues that the memo—*"yes, I got one of them in my in tray too, Bob!"*—was nothing more than a general warning shot across the bows from some nutcase—but maybe a very nice nutcase notwithstanding, I suggested. My smile probably came out as a lemon grimace or fingers dragging down teacher's blackboard like eight sticks of chalk. While the memo had pointed no fingers at anyone in particular (Bob might have guessed *someone* was trying to salvage his opus, but he had yet to identify more precisely *who* that someone might be). It contained a barely veiled threat to my ongoing and unfinished repair work.

Funnily enough, my initial suspicions as to the identity of the person looking over my shoulder at my literary endeavors had fallen not on Bob himself, but on Mr. Formaldehyde, neighbor and amateur taxidermist (*see* Hobbies and Pastimes). Mr. Formaldehyde's horrible, inaptly named living room (visible from the Hashes' own living room window) was adorned with a motley menagerie of deceased furry beasts, the centerpiece of which was a preternaturally calm marmoose, which thirteen falls back he'd brought home from a trip to Canada lashed to the roof of his car, its nostrils drooling on the windshield.

A few years back, from a makeshift laboratory he'd set up in his cellar, Mr. Formaldehyde had started up a small malodorous mail-order service operation, specializing in stuffed weasels. He dreamed of opening a big store with gleaming window displays in the mall downtown (*"Yes, we've got branches in New York, London, and Paris. What kind of weasel were you looking for, madame?"*) He imagined taking a trip to India to bag a tiger, or to the Arctic for a polar bear—must be big bags. His abiding ambition was to hunt down, bag, there's the word "bag" again, and stuff, the so-called Bird-Man of Easter Island, which, to my then paranoid ears, sounded more like *"messing around in the sawdust with which I will one day fill your gut."* Alas (except if you're a small furry animal such as a weasel), just as it seemed his mail-order business might get off the ground, the market for stuffed animals flattened out and went into terminal decline. Mr. Formaldehyde's business went bust. He was offered a job in the accounting department of Acme with quite reasonable remunerative prospects.

Even now in my new human guise, I couldn't but feel a certain unease in his eponymously smelly presence. For my liking, he was taking a little *too* much interest in the story of the window and the fate of Comenius. When he paid us a house call, I did not approve of the way he strummed on the bars of my empty cage. Had I not heard the rumor that Comenius the parrot—eight good handfuls of sawdust and a yard of fine-grade catgut—had dropped stone dead in his airspace? But, understandably wary as I might have been of Mr. Formaldehyde, I do believe we have a more obvious author for that memo to hand.

Before he eloped, Bob had given his final royal approval of the galley proofs, informing the master printer that there would "therefore be no need to check them again"—adding that he trusted Mr. Gleason might have them directly for their "speediest" publication, outlet distribution, etc. As per contract, the remaining two thirds of the advance, as well as all subsequent accruing royalties (as per terms of, etc.), were to be deposited directly to Miss Scarlett's Swiss bank account. And, to round off his arduous lexical labors (and basically to tie up the last loose ends of his dastardly scheme—till Commissioner Rex arrived on the scene), Bob had further announced that, as with immediate effect, he was going to take an extended sabbatical. With a theatrical, quite pointlessly cryptic tap on the window, he'd added: "Yes, Mr. Norton—I might be gone indeed for some time."

But however meticulous his planning, however thorough his preparations, Bob was not stupid: he knew there was always the risk of some unforeseen last-minute hitch. Had he really thought through *all* the possible outcomes? What if, on that fateful morning, waiting to pass through the gate for Acapulco, he suddenly decided that there remained in his fiendishly ingenious watertight foolproof plan one great big gaping loophole—

the possibility that Comenius had turned into his doppelgänger and would proceed in his absence to dismantle his shambolic *Forward with English!*—not to mention the hanky-panky the parrot might get up to with his wife? What if—a cartoon light-bulb pinging into surprise over his head and a palm slapstuck to his forehead—he and Señora Scarlett had ducked out of the line, doubled back from the airport, and taken "rooms" in some shady downtown lodgings in Bellville (neighboring town to bro-midian Belmont), where the landlady would turn a blind eye to the grammatical faux pas and marital credentials of her new tenants? And there lie low, just long enough to discount that absurd possibility about his parrot turning into his double, etc., make sure that, in all its bogus glory, the miscreant primer got safely into the bookstores; long enough to see that the errant compendium was up and stalking, cut loose from its creator— Belmont today, the world tomorrow—like an unstoppable Frankenstein's monster. After all, we did not wait to see him actually boarding that plane.

Even before Bob might have read that bland little article in the *Belmont Gazette* (the first tangible evidence that something was wrong on *Bob's* side of things), one can well imagine him, bunkered down within his day-curtained den, with the days ticking over and his glossy derangements failing to materialize in the bookstores, becoming increasingly concerned that something really *was* amiss with his plans: Miss Scarlett (today disguised in a frizzy peroxide wig and an old pink coat she'd found abandoned in the landlady's wardrobe) setting out on forays to the local bookstore, Bob thumbing impotently through a dogeared thesaurus to pass the time, only for her to return, like the dove, empty-handed. Why the delay? Why were his frivolous diffractions not in the stores yet as the printer had promised?

And now not only had the *Belmont Gazette* failed to mention the mystery—nay, scandal—that such an eminent disappearance as his, Bob T. Hash III's, should have created, it had had the gall to mention Miss Scarlett's, whether or not she was just on a ski trip. Why had missing fly posters not been glued to lampposts, to curbside trees, in both Belmont and Bellville? Why had search parties not been sent out to roam round the streets, roadblocks not set up on the outskirts of town? Why had vans not gone round with rooftop megaphone announcements, like the knife grinders of old? Why had an inflatable dirigible not cat-cradled to and fro over the city, Bob's noble, oblong face on the side, with a caption ribbon reading *Have you seen Bob T. Hash III?* trailing behind it. Why had his wife not made a tearful TV appeal?

Did nobody seem to think something just a *tad bit odd* that he'd not come back from his business trip? It was one thing to worry about a last-minute holdup with regard to the distribution of *Forward with English!* (eighth edition). But the lack of concern for his own disappearance—this was one factor Bob could *not* have foreseen.

I'm afraid all this business is beginning to take its toll on my health.

50

Say "Ah"—A Visit to the Doctor

Feeling a little under the weather one day, you drop in at your local general practitioner complaining of a stiffening of the forelimbs. Explain to the doctor (congenial half-moon glasses and obligatory stethoscope) that this is most likely the first sign of the onset of multiple sclerosis. Suggest that he make out a special prescription for medicinal cannabis that might bring relief to your muscular spasms.

A few days later you decide to pay another visit to the local clinic, convinced you have terminal cancer. Explain to the doctor that although you are unable as yet to indicate any precise manifestations, you feel sure that some nabilone derivative would make more bearable any symptoms that might in due course arise.

The next week you return again, this time with a suspected extremely exotic and highly contagious form of Parkinson's disease. According to a recently translated article published in the *New Belmont Journal of Medicine,* trembling and other side effects of this condition can be ameliorated through the use of medicinal marijuana. Discuss the article with your family physician, comparing the English translation with its Portuguese original. In particular, you might point out to the doctor (whose Portuguese is a little rusty) an important section in the original that has for some reason not been brought forward into the English version. According to this extirpated fragment, the prescription of cannabis brings not just relief to the patient but ensures immunity to the sufferer's prescribing physician.

This time you have the sniffles and a nasty cough. Although cannabis therapy has not yet in medical circles been put forward as a possible cure for the common cold, volunteer yourself as fearless pioneering guinea pig for cutting-edge (home-based) research into the potential beneficial effects of Sativex on its symptoms.

Once more you are shown politely, firmly, and another time empty-handed to the door. However, on your way out at the doctor's reception, ask Nurse Scarlett, since the doctor has once again run out of prescription slips, if she could just write one out for your refill medication.

"Just take this to the pharmacist's, Mr. Hash," says Nurse Scarlett, handing you the prescription. "And make sure you get plenty of rest!"

51

The question was how near Bob really was to piecing together the full picture. Reviewing now a series of events in light of the ominous memo, it looked like he was in fact a good deal nearer than I might have wished for. There was the business of the jacket at the dry cleaners. There was that ridiculous long lost twin turning up as milkman. There was that coincidence with the golf bags at the airport. More than once correspondence in the office appeared to have been intercepted—letters steamed open at the staff kitchen kettle before landing in my in tray. In Venice, at night, under honeymoon moonlight, the egregious hoaxer had tried to frighten me off by trotting along foggy canal walks in a crimson red duffel coat, matching red storm cap, and a fisherman's Wellington boots—all hopelessly several sizes too small for him. On the golf course, several of my registered holes-in-one had unaccountably been transmuted into bogies by the time I arrived on the green. From a dimly lit corner of the French restaurant I had been spied on from two almond-shape eyeholes cut into a rustling copy of the previous day's *Le Monde*. On Matilda's birthday, the UPS van that drew up to deliver my magnificent cattleyas deposited from an anonymous admirer an identical blooming bunch of flowers.

And now, hot off the press: this. As part of my research (yes, that's right, Bob, research) to help me rehabilitate the above *petit déjeuner pour un chien* into a once more fit state of health (presented again in Bob's bogus version—which I trust would have tickled drug-crazed hepcats and two-penny hedonists alike), I had myself limped along to the local clinic (armed as always with my policeman's notebook) for a brush with the world of bedpans, clip charts, and drips. Having taken a morning's worth of notes, I thanked both medics and nursing staff for their cooperation, French-kissed a couple of the nicer nurses, lobbed in a couple of puns to console the afflicted, thanked all for their often invaluable suggestions, and made saunter for the exit.

But, on my way out, I happened to notice a man on a waiting room chair, slouched as sick as a parrot. He had about him an "air of an Iberian"—and would no doubt within minutes be diagnosed as a victim of the Spanish flu. Please note that Bob is neither the first nor the only mortal being since the appearance of organic sentience on the planet to have suffered ill health.

52

American English vs. British English

Dan Smith from the London office is in Belmont to discuss the new motivational strategy with his American colleagues. After a day of busy meetings, Dan follows his colleagues into the office kitchen for some well-earned refreshment, only to find there are no more beers in the icebox (*Br. Eng.: "no more toby ales in the fridge"*). Chester and Janet from accounts decide to take Dan out for a night on the town.

Some more examples:

- these days I take the elevator = these days I take the lift ("all part of my new healthy lifestyle, Bob!")
- automobile = traditional steam train
- financial leverage (MIT) = "tandem" economics (Cambridge)
- fedora hat = trilby
- I say gas . . . you say oxygenious petrol
- vacational faucet garbage = rubbish holiday tap

- a howdie dawdi doodle do Stetson (another species of hat) = cricketer's bowler
- Señor Gonzalez watched the long line of people passing through the gate at the airport = long *queue* of people
- James Dean salad dressings and Grand Canyon cigarette ads = Mrs. Gaitskill's recipe for homemade steam puddings
- schedule = schedule (pronunciation)
- homeland traffic crossing guard = lollipop lady
- gridlock blues harmonica Wite-Out = haywain punk on leafy Tipp-Ex hedgerow
- Look out, there's a wrench in the gears! = Look out, there's a spanner in the works!
- businessman's toilet kit = businessman's sponge bag
- That new air-conditioning system sure takes the cake! = That new air-conditioning system really takes the biscuit!

Note that sometimes there is no difference.

As the evening's revelries draw to a conclusion (Chester having dropped out early to get back to some unfinished homework) Janet looks up at the sky and points out the Big Dipper—right above the intersection with Main Street. Dan Smith, after a moment's incomprehension, smiles.

"Ah, you mean the Great Bear, Janet! I'll soon get the hang of that," he says.

"You're getting the hang of it already there, Dan—welcome aboard!"

53

Who on a clear black night has not gazed up at that other con-
stellation, recently configured, the *Parrot*—incidentally, no differences astraddle the pond on that one—and wondered what
great consequences befell the narrator on the tails of the
surgery sighting (*Am. Eng.: "clinic"*)? I was able to deduce from
that little encounter, coming only a section or so after receiving
the mysterious fire drill memo, that a gauntlet had
been thrown down and that the stakes were high—
nothing less than the fate of *Forward with English!* Bob
had now, at the doc's, confronted his antagonist; I had confronted mine too. This was all about as plausible as an episode
of *Commissioner Rex*—the show about that dog I was telling
you about that thought it was Sherlock Holmes. But, like Rex,
Bob didn't need the full picture to know that his *Forward with
English!* could well already be in danger. Two twin Bobs had
looked at each other for the first time square in the eye. This
was war, a war on Bob. In the war of Bob against Bob, it was
like there was this one copy of *Forward with English!* being
lobbed back and forth between us like a book-shaped hot potato
in an animated cartoon. Only one of the versions was going to
become the new eighth edition—and if you dropped that hot
book-shaped potato it was most likely not going to be yours.

However much this was turning out to resemble a plot out
of *Commissioner Rex,* this last encounter did inject a
sudden urgency into my work as editor in chief. Hith-

erto, my idea of a deadline was but a rippling mirage in a heat haze. All at once, there was a race on to flush out the aberrancies from the remaining sections, before Bob put two and two together (*coming next*—Comparatives and Superlatives). And I did not relish the thought of having to fend off a windmilling lawn-invading Bob from his throne.

Till now, most of my troubleshooting work on what was to become the one and only approved and published official version of *Forward with English!* (eighth edition) had been done at my office desk, formerly Bob's. Soon after taking up my post there at the start of this story, I realized the office chores I was expected to perform required little more than my token appearance—a handshake, a wave, and a smile. To show I was a boss who did things, I would sometimes poke my head in at a meeting: *Good idea, Stan, but why not let's just have another look at last quarter's sales figures first?* But even on busy days I usually had enough time to rattle off my daily self-set quota of expungements before the midmorning coffee break without being disturbed: *Quite frankly, Stan, I think to be incurring an outlay of that nature on a new set of windows at this part of the business cycle would be counterproductive. . . .* These were then typed up by Miss Happ and slipped sweetly from her lap into my in tray, ready for a hop-skip-and-a-proofread before the afternoon tea break—Miss Scarlett remaining, alas, on the police missing persons' list (either that or lying with her left leg in plaster at a mountain ski resort). In any eventual wittily composed acknowledgment preface, tagged on to a long list of more eminent references, there is going to be a nod in Miss Happ's direction of the old "*. . . indispensable, indefatigable for fifteen minutes, without whose long suffering, etc."* type.

All that had been very nice and leisurely but now those days were over. It was time to roll up my shirtsleeves, for a surge™ in the war against Bob. With the idea of notching up the repair pace a gear or two, I canceled nonessential meetings (*Sorry, Molly, but the overhead projector's playing up again*). I forewent lunch hours in the office canteen. (Miss Happ was again good

enough to put in as much overtime as I needed.) True to the
Hash-ian tradition, I started bringing an overflow of work home
in the evenings in that famous clasp briefcase, thinking I could
work at the children's living room desk—forgetting that the
family would be having a snack or reading a book, or taking
turns to switch on/switch off the TV, or taking turns to close and
open the drapes (*Yes, Betsy is closing the curtains!*): conditions
somewhat less than conducive to the studious concentration
that my editorial labors demanded. But a solution, as always,
was just round the corner.

On the Saturday afternoon after I'd received the nasty
memo, lawn mower as hushed as a RoboKaddy golf buggy, I had
just finished shaving the lawn into a rather verdant rainbow of
halms. I was putting the mower away into the backyard shed
(even though the Scarlet Pimpernel never had to do this) when,
halfway up that ramp (that yellow cartoon lightbulb pinging
into surprise above *my* head this time), it occurred to me that
this might be the place of greater peace and isolation I needed
for my lexical graft work. Inside the shed—bracing smell of
pinewood in the drudge-to-be's nostrils—it was dry and spa-
cious; a quiet little window gave serenely onto the west and
those lovely blood-red sunsets so particular to Belmont. It was
summer, and if I were to requisition the garden shed and con-
vert it into a place of literary labor, the garden would be pleas-
ant and cool in the evenings. Shrubbery would muffle my cries
of "Bingo!" my cries of "Eureka!"

That same afternoon a clutter of gardening and horticul-
tural instruments made gallant room for the work desk, which
the children helped me drag out from the living room. (*No
Betsy, your homework will just have to wait.*) A spare Anglepoise
lamp was commandeered from the house; a bunch of lined pads,
erasers, ink refills, and tinctures of Wite-Out were brought
home from the office stationery department in the CEO's pockets. And—get this—a jet-black carnivorous Webster barbecue
on rugged traction-style wheels was parked outside the shed
door like a London beefeater for time and direction and crows.

Those traction-style wheels had thus far been put to the test only on the patio flagstones but were suitable, apparently, for "the roughest four-wheel outdoor terrains"—a sport-utility barbecue, if you like, in which I might incinerate scorch-earthed discarded drafts, aborted efforts, and, more important, Bob's original apocrypha, chapter by chapter, as I worked my way through his bog standard *Forward with English!* I was concerned that such scabrous and potentially damaging teaching material, if not completely destroyed, might somehow manage to reconstitute itself, wending its way into less scrupulous hands than mine.

Having converted the tool shed into a place of literary labor—what I came to call my "correctorium"—from then on I was able to withdraw in the evenings after partaking of the family dinner, thereby adding several hours of solid repair work to my stint at the office, accelerating the pace of my labor and hopefully maintaining a one-step advantage over Bob. (Had my sudden predilection for dried fruits and nuts in the office canteen—*Yes, Jack. It's all part of my new healthy lifestyle!*—and a request, at home, that nut roast usurp the traditional meatloaf, rung some Acme alarm bell?) The downside of this development, of course, was spending less time with Matilda, and which, for the meantime at least, proved something of a partial eclipse of our long balmy "quality time" evenings of quality coitus. But I knew that with Bob closing in—the memo, the clinic, the trademark surge—it was only a question of time before he figured out the whole story—and it was imperative to clean up *Forward with English!* and have it delivered into print before Bob did. Like a studious Saint Jerome, I was simply going to have to put in the hours. There was no way around it (unless of course I got someone else to do it for me). The Matildian "uninterrupted course of ease and content" had been interrupted; there was pine in my heart.

It can hardly be a question of coincidence that the day after I'd started my new evening working regime in the shed that I realized I'd fallen in love.

54

Comparatives and Superlatives

Some examples:

Jane is *taller than* Bobby but *not as tall as* Betsy.
Miss Scarlett's typing abilities are *the best* in the office.
The garden shed is *more conducive* to serious work than
the living room.
Hibs are *better than* Rangers or Hearts.

In the following exercise choose the word from the available options to complete each sentence.

a) The sales figures for last quarter show the fourth consecutive increase. Last quarter's sales figures are the _____ ever! (best/most recent/forever and)

b) I'm really enjoying this exercise. I haven't had this much fun since last _____ (time we went to Disneyland/exercise/Tuesday's fire drill).

c) A five-iron hits _____ a seven-iron but not as far as a three-iron. (farther than/nearer than/golf club)

d)   Mr. Hash went on his honeymoon to Venice. He said it was _____ honeymoon he'd ever been on. (the most aquatic/the most honey-full/the most Venice-like)

e)   A turbo-charged eight-cylinder SUV is _____ than the average saloon car. (more environmentally friendly/less environmentally friendly/less saloon-car-like)

f)   Signora Brambilla said the gherkins were the _____ she'd ever tasted. (most delicious thing/most disgusting thing/least un-gherkin-like thing)

g)   Tushi said the office party this year was _____ than last year. (better/partier/more tiger-economish)

h)   It is _____ for a camel to pass through the eye of a needle than for a Bob T. Hash III to. (easier/No, thanks, I don't smoke!/using a pygmy camel)

i)   Falling from the fifth-floor window takes _____ than from the sixth. (quicker elevator/less lift time/breath of fresh air will do you a world of good)

j)   Our worldwide organization has operations in more than 44,000 countries and has a turnover in the region of a trillion dollars per annum: so it must be the _____ (biggest/turnoverest/how many was that again?) company in the world.

k)   Letting the workers install their own air-conditioning systems was the _____ mistake since sliced bread. (biggest/most air-conditioning related/most sensible)

l)   The eighth edition of the course book is a vast improvement on the seventh. This is the _____ English course I've ever taken! (Englishest/course bookist/most improved)

LANGUAGE TIP! The incautious use of a comparative may require hours of argument and disputation to restore an initial parity; a cavalier but misplaced superlative can lead to stool-hurtling barroom fisticuff brawls amidst sawdust and spittoons. Before using comparatives, student is therefore advised to avail himself of a battery of supporting evidence and justifications to back up his assertion. Ipso facto, superlatives should really only ever be ventured out of earshot of the hearer.

55

Falling in love—so unexpectedly, so out of the blue—was perhaps the *best* thing that had happened to me thus far in this
whole escapade. Again, don't get me wrong—I had enjoyed the
picture book banter, I had enjoyed the little power trip in the office with its insipid hellos and good-byes; I was still enjoying
my fun with Wite-Out and pen. Truth be told, I had even quite
enjoyed falling off the perch and tumbling onto the living room floor ready-dressed in a suit and necktie. But
falling in love with Matilda was a better thing still by a
long way.

I suffered from the famous symptoms—the glow, the over-
whelm, the seismic shift, the gestalt switch, the Johnson flag-
poleons and a pattering heart. I longed to behold her of an
evening strolling round Duck Pond, running through her comparatives and superlatives. I longed to regale her long into candlelit night with the story of her husband's elopement, the tale
of how I had sacrificed my ladder, mirror, and perch for the bet-
terment of mankind . . . *coo-ee, over here!: Comenius is alive and
kicking . . .*

But I remembered also that if I told her before I'd done with
my revision on the eighth edition of *Forward with English!* and
she didn't believe me, I risked putting the entire project in jeopardy, not to mention the romantic affair itself. How might I
begin to broach the subject, how phrase such a frog-
prince-ish absurdity: *"Darling, you remember how I*

asked you to embark on the nut roast?" And what if the news of the transmogrifying parrot freaked her out? What if she thought I was her original charlatan husband (gone now forever)—only gone a little mad? Raving that he used to be a parrot indeed! What if she renounced me—what if she went back to pining for her long and forever lost Comenius?

On balance, the sanity of *Forward with English!* was simply too big and important a thing to risk. For better or worse, its fate had been entrusted to my hands: the time wasn't right yet. With the great leaps of progress I was making in the correctorium, my gremlin-free version would in any case be soon in the clear. There would be plenty of time to muse on these events then with a couple of rocking chairs up on the veranda and a fat rap-cat joobie Cuban cigar.

For the meantime I'd be like Orpheus, descended into a bright Tupperware hell to retrieve his Matilda—the condition being not that I can't look her in the face (e.g., as she waves me in from the veranda), but that I mustn't let her know I'm the parrot till I've rid *Forward with English!* (eighth edition) of her husband's misleading mischief once and for all—and got it safely off to the printers.

56

The Usual Suspects
the past progressive

Inspector Marlow is investigating a crime. A man has been found dead outside the Belmont office building of the Acme International Institute of Languages in Belmont. So severe were the injuries incurred that it has not so far been possible, nor may it ever be, to identify the deceased. The police have yet to decide whether to treat this as a case of mishap, suicide, or homicidal murder. Observing however that a fifth-floor window lies ajar, and privately suspecting foul play, Inspector Marlow decides to conduct a series of interviews in order to eliminate various persons as suspects from his inquiries.

Inspector Marlow's chief aim is to find out what the suspects were doing between the hours of six thirty and seven thirty on Friday evening, the inferred time of the incident. He asks each suspect, "What were you doing at seven o'clock on Friday evening?" which, expressed in the past progressive, means effectively, "What were you then *in the middle of* doing at that time?" In the following exercise, pair off the names in the box with the suspects' answers to the inspector's question below. The first one has been done already to help you:

> Warren Crosby; Lucinda, the Ping-Pong champion;
> Señor Gonzalez; Matilda; the Horologist; Mr. Gleason,
> the printer's assitant; Tushi Moto; Janitor Bert; Mick
> Aldehyde; You; Miss Scarlett

a) "I was taking down the bunting in the office foyer." (Janitor Bert)

b) "I was browsing at the Barnes and Noble for books about skiing."

c) "I was unwinding in front of the news on TV."

d) "I was remantling the birdcage in the living room."

e) "I was driving home from the office."

f) "I was setting a six-point Harrington typeface for the *Belmont Gazette*."

g) "I was mixing the sawdust for the Bird-Man of Easter Island."

h) "I was playing in the semifinal of the Belmont Ping-Pong championships."

i) "I was winding the clocks up."

j) "I was lying in my hammock and smoking a Cuban cigar."

k) "I was fornicating with his wife—so it can't have been me!"

Note that there may not necessarily be any causal connection between these actions and the victim's defenestration; any apparent synchronicity may be purely gratuitous. It is highly unlikely the deceased actually waited for any of these things to happen to tip him in favor of making a jump, nor (in the case of homicide) did the murderer see them as a signal to push, etc.— for which the simple past form would be used in place of the past progressive (e.g., "When I wound the clocks up, the man jumped out of the window").

Now put the alibis into order of plausibility, giving reasons. State who in your opinion has the least credible alibi and have them brought down to the police station for further questioning by the inspector.

57

Mirroring Bob's own "disappearance," I can imagine this implausible exercise turning up among a pile of clothes—a *Big Boss*™ business suit—discarded above the tide-line of a gigantic curve of shallow white sand (a schooner on a glistening calm horizon with a parrot in the crow's nest aboard)—discovered presumably by the student, taking his dog for a walk on Sunday morning in the gray light of dawn. (*"No, Rover, leave that alone. Here, that jacket looks like it's been cut from a fine bolt of cloth . . ."*). And, not unlike the implausible contrast there between glistening and gray, it's the very sort of stuff to drive any sane, mild-mannered African gray up the plastic multicolored rungs of the nearest ladder.

Funnily enough (to employ the contrast of tenses herein recommended), it was while I was reworking the past progressive (out there in my correctorium, pining for Matilda) that I first became aware of an insidious collateral hazard—that even once I'd eliminated them, even once I'd incinerated them in the barbecue (*"Another barbecue there this evening, Bob?" "That's right, Chuck. Just thought I'd rustle up a burger"*), some of Bob's homespun miswirings might still find a *very mysterious* way back into *Forward with English!* (eighth edition). Time again for the yellow lightbulb to ping into surprise over my head, a halo of cartoon thumbtacks: however braced one might be, it's not always easy to resist falling under the spell of Bob's impish perversions—especially when casting around for replacement phrases and one's critical faculties are overcome by a mind-blowing sense of possibility.

One can envision a lesser editor than Comenius, worn down by decaffeinated titter, permitting a Hash-ism to remain now here, another now there. Before you knew it, Bob's haywire aberrancies would be strutting back into *Forward with English!* like a flock of prodigal peacocks, back onto a croquet lawn from their lair in the willows—with the inevitable cavalcade of garish potpourrifications in tow.

I am happy to announce that Comenius has at all times managed to resist this munificent temptation.

58

Palindromes

Parrot cast its actor rap
Tar by tram, arty brat!
Drawn, one Polly did idyll open onward
Leek never, even keel
Flay ram alack calamary, Alf
Red? Now plug divot, Ovid—Gulp! Wonder!
Abracadabra: scenic Sotades abased at oscine csar—bad
    acarba!
Wend no maid a diamond new
Sub in moon, Bob: no omnibus
Bird mirror, or rim drib?
No, Sir Psittacid Daddi Cat, 'tis prison!
etc. etc.

LANGUAGE TIP! As far as possible, try to avoid using palin-dromes in everyday direct speech.

59

No, Bob, you eponymous little palindrome, I'm afraid this will just not cut the mustard. That "tar by tram," that "bad acarba," that "Psittacid Daddi Cat" indeed—surely not *the* Florentine muralist? Pah! Who among my symmetrical detractors *now* cannot crave the swiftest removal of Bob and his remaining cuckooisms (if I might be permitted—just this once—to coin something off my own bat)?

The budding linguist will be relieved to learn that I will be seeing this business through to the end. Things are now at last in capable talons and this as I've said is my surge. Soon, *nothing more will be left of Bob's antics* than a Cheshire cat's floating grin in the bough of a tree. No incompetent Sideshow Bob I.

I wonder, though, if there's not another danger here—that my revision work is now going *too* fast? Since setting up my correctorium, my work has come to acquire the impetus of a hare to bring the new eighth edition of *Forward with English!* to a definitive close. Only a few sections to go now till it gets sent off to the printers. But have I considered the possibility that once the job's done, my services might actually no longer be required? (Not that there's any real reason why I *shouldn't* carry on, in a noneditorial capacity—I'm really just exploring the possibility that my remaining in human form—and, more important, remaining Mrs. Hash's husband—might somehow be linked to my remaining in a troubleshooting role.) My mission completed, I might simply be withdrawn from the scene, no explanation given, as by a puppeteer's invisible hand, or when Superman—the inferno extinguished, the damsel returned to the ground (*"Let's just say it's good to have both feet back on the fifth floor!"*)—modestly blends back into the crowd of office workers gathered behind the police cordon (office geeks from the early sixties in short sleeves and neckties, throw in the odd trilby).

Shouldn't I maybe try to slow things up, postpone eventual completion, by undoing a little of each day's literary labor, just in case?

Talking of cops, besides inheriting Bob T. Hash III's deck of business cards, platinum this, identify that, all in Bob's name, all eminently valid (*"here, darling, look, a library card too"*) the title deeds to his house and his wife, I happen to have in my possession the author's rights to nothing other than the manuscript of *Forward with English!* (eighth edition)—not to mention the suspicious manuscript itself.

By the way, two more crates of celebratory fizzy pop and a carton of something soft were delivered this morning to the staff quarters' kitchen.

60

Idiomatic Expressions and Phrasal Verbs

Example: Those clocks seem to be slowing down. A horologist (whiskers, magnifying glass, and a very large clock key) has been summoned and is now trying to do something about restoring time to its usual velocity—in both the staff quarters' kitchen and elsewhere. We say of the clocks that the horologist "is *winding* them up."

In this exercise you have to choose the correct word from the lists to fill in the blanks. The first one has been done for you.

a) You and Bob Calvert are having a tea break. You take two sugars and milk and drink from a blue cup and saucer while Bob has a company-sponsored red cup with milk and no sugar. You break off to answer a phone call and, distracted, pick up the red sugarless cup of tea by mistake. You take a sip or two and declare: "That is not my _____ of tea!" (sponsorship/cup/kettle)

The correct answer is "cup"—That is not my cup of tea!

b) On the eve of an important business trip you are repairing some slight hurricane damage to the garden shed.
Purblind Little Johnnie is helping you out by replacing a
plank of wood. He holds a nail between left thumb and
index finger, swings with great instinctive accuracy with
the hammer in his right. Complimenting him, you say:
"You've hit the nail on the _____!" (hammer/
thumb/head)

c) Bob is at the office canteen. He has asked for several
helpings of nut roast, to which he now attempts to add a
rather large gherkin, which, there being no room left for
it on his plate, rolls off onto the tray. We say: "Bob has
too much on his _____." (tray/mind/plate)

d) It is raining outside and Mr. Hash and the children
call off their game of Frisbee in the garden. They decide
to play an indoor game involving small round glass
transparent balls, threaded with threads of opalescent
color—onyx, amethyst, ruby. Having looked high and
low for the soft velvet pouch in which these little glass
balls are kept, he finally gives up. We say: "Mr. Hash
has indeed lost his _____!" (Frisbee/umbrella/
marbles)

e) Your wife has been doing breaststrokes in the local nata-
torium. She wishes now to come out and dry herself off.
With great promptitude and helpfulness from the side
of the pool you "throw in the _____." (kitchen
sink/water wings/towel)

f) It has been raining. You are inside, waiting to get on
with a game of tennis. You ask Mary to look out the win-

dow to see if it's stopped. You ask her to "take a
_____ check." (Mary/tennis/rain)

g) A wagon with faulty axle has failed to pass its road test
and has been banned by the sheriff from further road
usage until the problem is fixed. You decide you must
write a book and, as you see the wagon being towed off to
the scrap heap and everybody else seems to be doing so,
you find it irresistible not to "_____ on the banned
wagon." (test/jump/write a book)

h) There is a manila envelope on the desk. With your hand
you shunt it forward. Miss Scarlett, entering your office,
observes: "You're _____ the envelope." (posting/
watching/pushing)

i) To pass the time Mr. Hash and Miss Scarlett are playing
a game in the local municipal park. Mr. Hash throws a
short length of sturdy twig and Miss Scarlett runs to
fetch it. One of the rules is Miss Scarlett must pick it
up at the end with the leaf attached to it. This time,
however—breathlessly running back toward Mr. Hash—
she has clearly picked it up at the end with no leaf. "Miss
Scarlett has got the wrong end of the _____ ."
(leash/Bob/stick)

j) Bob and Jack are on a fishing trip. Bob has hooked a
lovely marlin. On the point of reeling it in, the line
snaps. Notwithstanding concerns of depletion due to
high levels of toxic effluence, one suspects that the
escapee marlin is not the last living example of its
species. Jack says: "Don't worry, Bob, there's plenty more
_____ in the sea." (water/fishing lines/fish)

k) A parrot, having been discovered at customs in a smuggler's suitcase, recounts the hallucinatory tale of his ad-

ventures. At the end of his tale the parrot then invites you to choose from a selection of Viennese chocolate, French cream cake, Battenburg, etc. You say: "I've heard some daft stories in my time, Bob, but that one really takes the _____!" (grammar book/suitcase/cake)

l) Bob is at the hippodrome, where he hired a very long-legged horse for an hour. It is now one hour and ten minutes since hire time began and, though a small queue of pegs has formed, Bob shows no sign of stopping. You say "It's time Mr. Hash got off his (trot/one-hour/high) horse—and I suggest he be taken down a _____ this very instant!" (short-legged horse/hippodrome/peg or two)

Some exercises are entirely without merit, and this is a nice example.

To enter, for a wild millisecond, into Bob's reckless idiomatic spirit, it could be said of our mischievous compiler that, with this latest exercise, he has finally "ventured forth from a bucolic rolling dale context and relocated himself in an urbanized focal point at the epicenter of the maddening concrete" (gone to town). It is high time indeed for us to "replace at a lower altitude, with firm determination, the extremity of one of our singular hind limbs" (put our foot down). *"Yes, Miss Ratcliffe, down at the front here; your homework on the dangled modifier came top of the class."*

Another two mysteriously light cartons (popcorn, balloons?) have been delivered to the staff office kitchen. This was the major (external) event of today. There's no point complaining. Let us carry on without further comment, and proceed to the next section.

Lodging a Complaint

"*N*o, *I don't read much these days. I don't have as much time as I used to.*"

Bert has returned from the Belmont branch of Barnes and Noble with a book. Presently he settles down in his favorite armchair to read it by the light of a lamp. After a few pages he decides to put down the book and see what's on TV.

Sometimes the goods and services we purchase do not meet with our unqualified approval. We encounter unforeseen imperfections, we feel let down in our expectations, a snort will escape from the nostrils—first steps along the road to a more pervasive disaffection.

Homework assignment!
Student has to imagine he is Bert and has to compose an irate, rambunctious letter to the regional manager of the Barnes and Noble bookstore in Belmont, expressing—in no uncertain terms—his disappointment with his purchase, asking

for an assurance that this sort of stuff will not appear in the shop window ever again. The letter of complaint will take the form of a dust jacket blurb, which student feels more accurately represents the book than the blurb that persuaded him to buy the book in the first place. By special agreement with the management of the bookshop chain, the publishing house in question has kindly agreed to forthwith replace the existing blurb with student's suggested alternative, with immediate effect. The bookstore will let the student choose between a refund, exchange, or some form of token. In certain cases, the house in question will be happy to pulp the book directly upon publication.

"Yes, I've taken up reading too. It's quite trendy these days!"

.

63

How often did I myself not stop to admire that glittering window display at the Belmont Barnes and Noble.

Only a few days ago—yesterday, in fact—I was returning to the office from the menswear department of the super new multistore with a nice new sober necktie. It was still in its box, not around my neck yet. When I was buying it, I had the idea of getting Matilda a little surprise, so I was now making a beeline for the bookstore. Outside, their beaks, I mean noses, pressed against the bookstore pane, a little crowd had gathered. What frolicking roll-call we could have here of the Mother's Days, Father's Days, Christmas days, Easter Sundays, Valentine's Days, back-to-schools, Halloweens, High-Five Days, Thanksgivings, Labor Days, Mardi Gras days, and any number of other suchlike saturnalian dispensations—commemorated so diligently by the bookstore proprietors in that window display space. I went up to join the little crowd. There behind the vast pane of reflect-proof (and, who knows, bullet-proof?) plate glass was a studious-looking mannequin of Bob T. Hash III in pajamas, a tweed-checkered bathrobe, and a pair of matching slippers. To the left of the fire tongs, and leaning against the side of the mantelpiece clock, were—no, stop rushing me—not piles of *Forward with English!* (the new eighth edition), but, rather, a murder mystery—what Ragioniere Brambilla would call a *giallo*. The cover had a woman in a red dress outside a window—a sort of fluttering

flambé femme fatale. There was a copy in the mannequin's
lectern hand. His elbow resting on the mantelpiece of an avuncular hearth side, the mannequin was reading away at it while
puffing on his Sherlock Holmes pipe.

But look, Rex—did that page not turn on its own? Was not
that wisp of fake smoke in bromidian motion after all? Did not
that eyebrow rise when it spied my arrival?

I did not linger long. I did not make a purchase. I did not go
back to the office. I proceeded forth to the correctorium on the
swiftest of casters.

64

"Could Have Done"/ "Was Going to Do"

The past of "could" (do, be, etc.) is "could have" (done, been, etc.). We use "could have done" to say that we had the ability or the opportunity to do something, but that we did not in the event actually do it. This is related to "wanted to (do/be, etc.)," meaning "I desired something but was prevented (thwarted by circumstances, by fate, etc.) from achieving it," and is also related to "was going to (do, etc.)," which we use in situations of aborted projects, where we perhaps set out with the best of intentions that for our own good reasons we elect to abandon before reaching completion. For a more emphatic sense of regret (the infamous "kicking oneself") use "should have (done)" or, conversely, "should not have (done)."

Some assorted examples:
a)   At the airport shop in Prestwick, Bob could have bought himself a brand-new set of Waverley

persimmon-shafted blackthorn woods with
tartan cozies, a full set of Rob Roy irons
including the famous "Black Duncan" mashie, a
Ballantyne Club-Pro mutton-crested golf bag
with sporran holders, half a dozen MacGregor
clan peat-resistant polyhedric golf balls, a packet
of indomitable Abbotsford golf tees, a wee tartan
Tammie, and an Old Morality hip flask. (=but
did not)

b) Matilda could have taken up the
pianoforte/xylophone/lute, etc. (=would now be an
internationally renowned concert
pianist/xylophonist/lute minstrel, etc., but didn't, so
is not)

c) Mrs. Thomson went to the ball. She could have
danced all night.

d) Oops! I should have posted that manila
envelope.

e) Dan should have taken up Spanish lessons before he
arrived in Madrid. (=it was imprudent of him to set
off linguistically unprepared. On arrival in Madrid
he decided he wanted to go back to Belmont to take
that course of lessons after all)

f) Mrs. Novák was going to have a quick bath before
her guests came for dinner—but did not.
(=barefooted, wrapped in a nice toweling bathrobe—
discovering the carp in the bath)

g) The dwarf chef should have put processed cheddar
cheese in the croque instead of Gruyère. (=the
opinion of roving globe-trotter and bon vivant Bob T.
Hash III)

For irredeemable and unalterable events, cast in marble
and lost to the mists of time, the past simple is to be preferred.
Note that in English there is no "remote past" form: no gram-

matical distinction is made between something that happened
five minutes ago and something that happened, say, during the
late Cambrian period, epoch of cuttles.

*"There exists indeed a breed of grammatical construction for
which . . ."*

65

Case in point, I *could* have left that manila envelope alone in the out tray without looking inside it. Even better: I *should* have let the manila alone. I should have let the manila lie there in the out tray till it got taken off by the postal staff. I could have rustled up a cup of coffee and looked out the window with my feet up on the desk instead. But no, like an idiot parrot, I had to fish the thing out. That was the fork in the path. Yes, it's true—head nodding ruefully—if I'd let that manila alone, none of this course book repair stuff would have happened. I can tell you, if I'd left that manila alone, I'd be living out the life of Riley by this stage. I'd have built a pool in the garden. I'd have taken up Spanish and extended that range of executive toys on my desk—blissfully indifferent to the virus of Bob's trademark would-be-ubiquitous McLitespeak around me. I would not have this extra workload on my plate (*Forward with English!*, eighth edition) with its partial eclipse of Matilda, glowing red like the moon or that fluttering flambé femme fatale. And, more to the point, Bob would not now be closing in on me with murderous intentions. . . .

(By the way, that "There exists indeed a breed of grammatical construction for which . . ." would appear to be a fragment detached from some larger body of work. One is struck by its air of apparent freestanding integrity. For a long time it had nowhere to go. It has been shoved here for no good reason at all.)

A solution must be found: either I go back into the past in a time machine and reposition the manila envelope in the out tray, or I kill him off now. Or, vice versa, Bob kills me off. Even as I write this sentence, he's probably working out the best moment to make a dramatic return, hoping to reclaim the role he not long ago so cynically spurned. I suppose if Bob hadn't been closing in on my reparation work, I *could have* spent a few moments telling you about the recurring nightmare I've been having lately—germane here on account of its no doubt being the result of a slight congestion of *petite trouvaille* in my slumbering corrections-yet-in-progress-addled brain.

In this nightmare, I could have told you, I am still Bob T. Hash III and I still work in the Acme office on Main Street—the difference being that my colleagues and I no longer seem to share the same language. My *Please, Miss Happ, when we're ready, if we could just take that dictation* and my *Hey, Jack, did you get a chance to read that report of the quarterly sales figures?* fall on double Dutch ears. A small crowd of colleagues gathers around me, like I'm some kind of freak show. Oh, nòt with any menace or anything, no medieval cudgels or flaming torches (bearing in mind, apart from anything else, I'm in theory, still their boss)—more a with a sense of well-meaning curiosity, prodding me with gentle questions. Probably they're asking to be told what to do. *I'm ready for that dictation whenever you're ready, Mr. Hash,* rendered in some weird exotic foreign babble-tongue. And I think to myself in this dreamworld why can't they just learn McLitespeak and be done with it? Don't they know life is too short (especially if your name happens to be Bob T. Hash III)? My colleagues stand around me in a circle, taking turns trying out different languages on me (even though they might just have been on holiday someplace or taken up a night class in it) like they're playing some kind of competitive game of who can guess which language I'm speaking. Since no one guesses correctly, none of them wins and they return to their desks.

By the inscrutable logic of dreamworlds, I realize that the English language has somehow been reduced to a withered, dialectical rump, spoken only by a remote enclave of insular, illiterate, umbrella-brandishing, bowler-hatted, octogenarian goatherds—and by me—and is on the brink of demise. In order that communication between myself and my colleagues can be restored once more to the free-flowing exchange of ideas and mellifluous understanding it once was, it is decided that I be steam-enrolled on a total immersion, fast-track, Pap intensive in Pap-trap McLitespeak (levels 1–2). (My protests that it is *they* who should be taking language courses, not I—since they're the ones who've decided, collectively, apparently overnight, to all start speaking in another language—fall, of course, on deaf ears.)

Luckily they've got nice new tables and chairs in the classroom and a smiling secretary at the front desk who says hello in the language of your choice just like at Acme! I learn fastly! Picking up not only the lingo itself but absorbing the mores and customs of a strange and distant people, as if by osmosis. Miss Porlock, if I might single her out, having picked up her towel, is particularly full of praise: "Bravo, bravo. Fastly, fastly, Bob T. Hash the third. Bravo, bravo. Fastly, fastly, Bob T. Hash the third!"

But true to nightmare scenarios, it seems no matter how well I progress in my new language in one night's dream—and I do feel, along with Miss Porlock, that I'm making good headway—when I have the same dream the following night, I find I've not retained even the most basic smattering of the new language I was doing so well in. I must enroll once again, back to lesson one, page one, *"This is a book. This is a chair. . . ."* But of course by next night again, that progress too, like Martin Finnegan's whiskers, all down the drain. . . .

I wake. The dream is over. (If this had been happening to Bob—as I suspect it was meant to—then one could see a certain

Dantean taste-of-your-own-medicine logic to it.) To show for my night class efforts I have nothing but the odd logofied Biro, or pamphlet telling me how easily I will pick up the new language—sad souvenirs brought back from my dreamworld. (Well, that or maybe just inadvertently brought back from the office in a CEO's pocket?) It's just after six fifteen on the digital alarm clock. The grapefruit sun will be rising out of reed-bordered Duck Pond on the outskirts of Belmont.

I lie there on the cool silken sheets, listening to the dawn chorus, an arm draped languidly over Matilda's frilly lace-trimmed apple pies (tried on in the lingerie department of the department store on an alas expurgated Question Tags section). No need to worry about us there, darling—*we* speak the same language. . . .

"Oops, is that someone inside the wardrobe?"

66

Tendering a Resignation
"I can't go on. I must go on."

Sometimes we find ourselves in a situation we no longer deem tenable and as a consequence believe we are unable to continue.

Note to the instructor: Ask students to think of a position from which they would wish to resign. For homework get students to write a letter to the relevant personnel department (human resources) requesting formal termination of the relevant contract and the severance of all ties ("to whom it may concern . . ." "more time to spend with Mr. Hash's family," "pursue outside interests," etc.). Next lesson have students read out their letters in a loud clear voice—from a precarious dais or improvised pedestal for dramatic effect—to the rest of the class. Students should be encouraged to use upbeat language and tone in this exercise. Teacher shows class picture of gold watch and commemorative chain. A small brass band and sponsor's bunting can be arranged on request.

You may like to use some of the following situations. Please bear in mind that while typical, the list should not be considered exhaustive.

a) As executive tycoon and CEO of a major importer of spare components for dishwashers, you feel that your talents are largely underutilized. In a letter to the board, request truncation of contract as with immediate effect, explaining that it is time to move on and seek out fresh challenges more in line with your abilities and natural ambition. . . .

b) Under your tenure as production manager at the Caxton and Tally-ho! printers plant, print runs of shoddy teaching material have been widely distributed on a worldwide scale . . .

c) As production manager at Jackdaw Asbestos Inc., you have allowed badly maintained and rusty equipment to slow down levels of output, resulting in a sustained loss of retail orders. Despite recent warnings, you have shown little enthusiasm for turning things round. . . .

d) As customs and baggage officer at Belmont International Airport, you are responsible for the shifts during which, among other things, two sets of golf clubs have been sent spinning round the world in the wrong direction, and a potentially dangerous parrot smuggler has managed to pass through customs undetected. . . .

e) You have been having a rampant affair with Bob's wife.

You were right, Jack, that new temp we employed is just not up to the job. I'm expecting her resignation letter to plop into my in tray any day now!

67

This exercise might provide another clue as to why Bob went to the bother of disguising himself as Señor Gonzalez on the way to the airport. While he'd been "working" on his version of the resignation section above, I had watched Bob write a letter of resignation himself, no doubt with the idea of testing out the effectiveness of his own templates for the course book exercises, but also—as his collection of miscreant persiflage piled up—with the idea of testing out an intuition he had about the kind of grip the Belmont picture book had on his own freedom of movement. By submitting a sort of draft hoax of a resignation, Bob would see the sort of reaction he'd get if he ever tried to resign in earnest. Expressing in his letter a sudden, unforeseen disenchantment, using in its composition an amalgam of the templates outlined above, Bob sent off his letter of resignation, and waited.

He envisioned the board being thrown into some kind of shock at the news that he, Bob T. Hash III, should even be thinking of resigning: a call to the boardroom for an informal chat and a brandy. Equally, he might have anticipated a laughing Jack Smith (R&D) coming into his office, letter open in paw, having caught its spirit of harmless prank: *"Sure thing, Bob! You know if we ever need to write a new course book, we sure could use some of this stuff!"* He expected it might take about a week for people to work out whether he was being serious, or sarcastic, or just a wee bit of both.

However, the very next day, the letter, apparently un-opened, was back in Bob's in tray. Perplexed, he sent it off again: probably just some mix-up in the mail room. But again, a day or so later, the letter bounced back, again apparently un-opened. This was strange. Bob stared at the envelope with a kind of horror and a feeling of entrapment. For in that dumb re-buff there was a point-blank refusal even to consider his re-quest.

Bob realized that if ever he *did* want to stop being Bob T. Hash, he was either going to have to wait for the institute to de-cide his services were no longer required (with the "keys to Bel-mont" in his possession, this might now be a very long wait) or he was going to have to quit in some dramatic way of his own devising (such as passing himself off as Señor Gonzalez and fly-ing off to Acapulco with Miss Scarlett).

Meanwhile, with regard to my own compositions (maintain-ing my vigilant 24/7 bulwark, like the little Dutch boy with his finger in the dam), I have made a point of writing to Mr. Glea-son, the printer's assistant, apologizing once again for the un-foreseen delay. I have reminded him that I am still working on those "eleventh-hour emendations." I have told him I'll have the definitive manuscript off to him the very second those amend-ments have been safely installed—assuring him it will be a matter of days.

68

The Good Samaritan: A Skit

In despair that his *Forward with English!* now lies in ruins, Mr. Hash is standing on the fifth-floor ledge outside his office window, preparing to throw himself off. Before climbing onto the ledge, Mr. Hash took the precaution of dialing the suicide hotline and, making use of the office extension cable, has brought the receiver with him onto the ledge, where he now stands amid bemused pigeons.

Student task: You are a volunteer at the Samaritan switchboard and have just received the distressed gentleman's phone call: your job is to persuade Bob to climb back into his office and get back to work. Student might like to be thinking of reasons why Mr. Hash should remain of this world, both general reasons and reasons specific to his particular predicament. You might also like to be thinking of alternative, less messy methods of killing himself—sort of backup suggestions should your first line of reasoning be rejected.

Note: Language instructor may like to have student acting part of Mr. Hash stand on a chair to enhance feelings of vertigo. More advanced students may appreciate more direct variants on the phone scenario where the Samaritan can be positioned either just inside the fifth-floor window (i.e., inside Mr. Hash's executive office itself) or alternatively standing muddy-footed below the window in an ornamental flower bed. Note subtle differences in tone and attitude between the three approaches and discuss them in class.

Meanwhile, yet another box of reinforcements has arrived in the staff kitchenette. Doesn't time fly! From an opened box, bottles of whiz-kid fizz have been transferred to the office refrigerator—*no, you first, sir, I insist*—icebox (*see* American English vs. British English). Ahead of schedule one ink-blue balloon has already been inflated and has been affixed—helium/Sellotape/involuntary floating?—to the ceiling. Thanks to my own philanthropic intervention, the above contribution and its ilk have now been done away with.

Our fifth-floor staff kitchenette is a convivial locus. It has a counter; it has mugs, plates, you name it. It has a cork-based notice board with ads for the Belmont marathon, and details for the upcoming sales figures announcement staff party on Friday. And—look, Miss Happ!—here's a new postcard from, let's see where, looks very nice, doesn't it, ah, yes, as I thought, it's from Acapulco (feel how the thumbtack's still warm): *"Wish you were here—looking forward to seeing you all at next week's sales party!"*

Comenius trusts that the very considerable personal risk to his life he runs by making these little commentaries will not be in vain.

A Dictation: Ordering a Coffin

To be read out to class by teacher. Select student with recent bereavement (if available) to read out in class after teacher.

"Last week Bob had to order a coffin. Warren at the office suggested he try Harry Dig the undertakers because when Grandmother Crosby passed away, he went there [comma] and got excellent service. "What you gonna put in there," said Warren like a cowboy, "potatoes?" Ignoring Warren's cryptic suggestion, Bob put on his hat and went down to Harry Dig's on Main Street. [Period—new sentence.] Inside Harry Dig's, Bob could smell freshly cut flowers as he browsed at the urns. Harry appeared from behind a drape of purple velvet. "How's tricks, Bob T. Hash III?" Harry said, extending a big welcoming, almost mafialike handshake, plus a leaflet detailing special schemes to save up for a coffin. [Open parenthesis] basically the sooner you thought about it the more you were going to save [end parenthesis]. "What kind of percentage region are we talking about here, Jack?" Bob said, even though he wasn't actually speaking to Jack at that moment. Or even to Harry Dig. He was speaking to the leaflet. But the point was he'd got the term "kind of percentage region we're talking about" bit in—which would look good in the primer. Bob did a sniff and took off his hat. Suddenly Bob said, "Good morning, I will soon need a coffin," this time to Harry, who replied that these things sometimes happen. "What's it for then, a sack of potatoes?" Harry said, if Bob would like to look through the catalogue and price list. Luckily the place had air-conditioning. There were photos of crosses and angels arranged not unlike some menus for foreigners with pictures of the dishes, so you just had to point. Bob said how difficult it was to decide, there was simply just too great a range of choices to choose from! But he gave Harry a clue regarding the sack of potatoes: the coffin was for his twin. "An identical twin?" asked Harry, his interest piqued. "I didn't know you had a twin." And Bob said yes it was indeed an identical twin, and I do. "What, did he turn up on your doorstep one day and drop dead on the spot?" said Harry as he took out his measuring tape to take Bob's measurements in the manner of a tailor and wrote down the numbers. "I'll take that nice one in the middle range then for those dimensions I gave you," Bob said. "How soon can you have it ready?" he added, as he put on his hat, familiar as it is in every household, stressing he had an early Monday morning tee-off. "That's a great air-conditioning system you've got there, Mr. Dig, by the way." "Why, thank you," said Harry, but then seeing that time was pressing upon time bandit Bob, he continued, "I'll get onto the casketsmith right away. For that sack of potatoes, or, as you put it, twin. And don't worry—as soon as it's ready, you'll be the first one to know!"

71

With this cheery lame little regurgitation, things continue their inexorable bovine backslide toward disaster. With Bob apparently on the brink of sussing out what his apparent, if anonymous, replacement (an angst-free Clark Kent Sisyphus in diamond-knit cardigan) was doing to his jumbled-up leavings, one could well see him taking advantage of the sales figures announcement and the celebratory chaos of its aftermath as the natural platform for a dramatic reentry. And much as Friday is being anticipated by management and staff alike (and I'm pleased for them, really, I am!), I find I am unable to partake of that enthusiasm myself. (*"No, Miss Janet, I'm fine. Just got a bit of a headache. Thanks, I've already taken one—it should be kicking in any minute now."*)

As I thought I had dealt with the dictation, it did not help that I was to find a most unwelcome message waiting for me when one morning I arrived at my office. The moment I saw the flashing light on my voice mail, a sixth sense told me something was wrong—nobody leaves messages in the middle of the night. Well, at least not in Belmont. I laid the *Gazette* down and gingerly picked up the receiver. I listened as the technology clicked in—Bob's (original) voice telling how he wasn't in his office right now, but if the caller left a message, he'd get back as soon as, etc. . . . another wave of beeps and a click for the start of the message.

It was Miss Scarlett, in her anchor-and-knot scarf.

At first there was just silence, and a few nocturnal ahms and erms: you could palpably hear her deciding whether or not to leave a message. When she did speak, Miss Scarlett spoke in a whisper, not a long-distance whisper from Acapulco, nor even Bellville—it sounded more like she might've been calling from one of the coin booths outside the mall. "Mr. Hash, Mr. Hash, please pick up the phone if you're there! Have you found it, Mr. Hash? Have you looked in the files yet?"

Then just rain in the background till the line went dead with a click and a purr.

A little bird tells me that life is but brief.

72

Take Me to Your Leader: A Role Play

Earth has been invaded by a troop of strange beings from outer space who, despite a limited command of English, appear to be benign: these are the Limbo Martians. Their spaceship, a very large silver-white Frisbee-shaped saucer, has landed on the thirteenth green of the golf course on the outskirts of Belmont.

Returning from an afternoon training seminar picnic held in a nearby township (Bellville), you and your fellow passenger colleagues, alarmed by the blaring soundtrack of the spaceship's unearthly eddying throb, decide to "interrupt schedule," and pull up at a safe distance. Through a gap in a hedgerow you observe that a group of Limbo Martians have descended a ramp protruding from the rim of the spaceship and are now gathered in a pool of humming blue light round their leader.

Note to the instructor: For the following skit task [particularly suitable for larger classes] you will need a volunteer Col. Hash, a lead Limbo Martian, and an offstage Bob T. Hector Hash.

Skit

As Astronaut Hash you have been selected to represent the earthlings and it is your job to persuade the Limbo Martians to take up a six-month trial course in Beginner's Business Essentials in English (at a special introductory rate).

As part of your approach you might like to set up trestle tables on which are arranged vast quantities of course material not unworthy of Patroclus's funeral celebrations: course books, business cassettes, logo-encrusted ballpoint pens, lucky dip key rings, and progress clip charts. Javelin contests, chariot races, animal sacrifices, drinking contests, commence. Bonfires burn late into the night.

DISCUSSION: Why might the Limbo Martians have chosen Earth as their planetary destination as opposed to other available planets in other solar systems with perhaps more abundant reserves of natural resources, more binary-oriented language systems, and more convivial inhabitants at their disposal? Discuss the myriad ways in which improving the space people's English might allow them to leapfrog ahead of their fellow stay-at-home Limbo Martians on return to their own distant planet.

73

In all probability, Bob's so-called Limbo Martians were members of the local acting society who'd been dolled up in aluminium foil, Scotch tape, and beekeeper masks. The saucer was probably nothing more than an obscenely oversize touring camper some crapulous fat cat had driven onto the seventeenth fairway, mistaking it for his front lawn—now that does sound familiar. The supposed Patroclesian celebrations, for their part, were more likely a sprawling soft-fisticuff-and-cupcake-barbecue mêlée between disgruntled nocturnal golfers and a group of bedraggled do-gooders from the local book club, the numbers made up by the Belmont district constabulary—all expertly choreographed by director Bob T. Hash III, and limned in his so-called researcher's sketchpad.

I have noticed, as many fellow travelers will have also, a similarity in tone and content, a certain felicity in timing, a certain parroting, if you will, between the above exercise and a silly story that appeared earlier this summer in the *Belmont Gazette*. Summer being typically the season, in Belmont as elsewhere, when stories are sparse, and newspapers have to make up things for themselves (like that Miss Scarlett disappearance). Anyway, according to the article in question, so-called exotic avians are in the process of "taking over" the local parks of our beloved Belmont. Having escaped through their owners' windows, a number of budgies, lovebirds, parakeets, lorikeets (not to mention domesticated parrots with unwieldy vocabularies that keep putting things in parentheses) are now not only able to survive at our hitherto inclement latitudes but, thanks to global warming, are now able to breed with free abandon in the now increasingly more gentle climes of our native city parks, formerly intemperate, now simply peppered with tree-perched pointillist daubs of Day-Glo oranges and twittering prismatic crimsons. Small feral colonies are now being observed, reproducing in conclavian miniature their natural subtropical habitats, to the best of their abilities. The story was accompanied by a map of the park in question replete with little hash signs (#) to show density of bird.

An in-depth inside article took up the theme. With due gravity, the voice of the *Belmont Gazette* informed us that although the park-bird phenomenon was quite serious in Belmont itself, it was not by any means restricted to Belmont alone. It has been observed in bromidian Bellville, for instance, and even farther afield. Agricultural scientists and apiculturists—no, that's bees—aviaptologists (*"Thank you, Matilda, with you in a sec"*) are warning not only of a threat posed to the indigenous species (starlings, blackbirds, cardinal tits) in terms of food stock, nesting rights, etc., but the fascinating possibility that, since they— the exotic birds, that is—are no longer restricted to the role of mere in-house mongers of living room entertainment (microwave tings, embarrassing expletives in front of auntie), our feathered and re-feralized friends (notably the African gray, or *Psittacus erithacus*) might make use of the language of their former masters to communicate among themselves, in a gregarious fashion, to the vertiginous level of *advanced certificate*—as defined by Acme International Institute of Languages, Main Street, Belmont (CEO unavailable for comment).

Ah, *the caged bird will sing*—nice comfy thought that, for wistful timid souls!

74

"Un Piccolo Incidente al Crematorio . . ."

(Another chance to practice your Italian!)

Scene: the town crematorium. Deceased: Patroclus Hash, husband, father, cuckold, pedagogue, manqué bungee jumper. Weather: rain. Dress: black suit and tie; umbrella preferred. You find yourself in a back-row pew of the gathered mourners. As the short grammatically unimpeachable eulogy nears a conclusion, you recall with a start the deceased once mentioning (in a jovial, offhand manner over drinks in the clubhouse) how he suffered from a rare "faux rigor mortis" syndrome wherein under certain circumstances—for example, suffering from a concussion—the sufferer appears for all intents and purposes to be dead when in fact he's in some kind of narcoleptic coma.

Role play 1) You take the role of the concerned mourner. Springing forth from the rear of the chapel as the service is nearing its climax, try to have urgent words with presiding priest.

Role play 2) You play the role of Noberto, an obdurate furnace hand. This being vacation employment for which—on paper at least—the spoken word is little needed, your linguistic talents have not yet been stretched much beyond arranging the occasional romantic assignment, and you are alas little able to understand what the frantic mourner who has come round to the furnace area is trying, apparently so desperately, to tell you.

Only Italian is to be used in these role plays. Students should feel free to use appropriate hand gestures in the traditional Italian manner. (Alternatively, more advanced students can have their hands tied to their sides to prevent them from doing this.) Please note that during this exercise teachers have been asked to enforce the strictest zero-tolerance policy toward any manhandling whatsoever of the coffin.

Here are some phrases the student might find useful:

Qui hic minxerit aut cacarit habeat deas superos et inferos iratos! = Here minx hick at cassarit, has two superb irritating infernals

Tieni i tuoi cavalli . . . é stato cremato solo il tuo sosia! = Hold your cavals! We've only cremated your sosies!

Attento, non toccarla, che ti bruci le dita!—non appoggiarsi . . . = Don't touch her there with your finger!—no apogees . . .

farfalle (93), pasta di semola di grano duro; cottura dodici min, diece al dente = far-falling smells of pasta at gran's door, you're a cot (93)

Eccoci! Le ceneri, sono pronte. Aspetti un attimo che trovo l'urna adatta . . . = Here, sir, your ashes are pronty. Aspects an a team that works the adopted urna

una fenice . . . un pappagallo, invece = a fence? . . . no, a papal gale invoice

And finally, as the furnace hand relents, upon opening the casket, you declare, somewhat aghast:

"Acciderboli! Sembra che qualcuno ha rubato la salma!" = *"Crivens! Same bra call has rubbed the lady salmon!"*

75

"It is men we are forming, not parrots."
—J. A. COMENIUS

I like to think of myself as having been present at the time and place that the eighth edition of the Acme institute's well-loved *Forward with English!* sprang into life. I was right there at the glint in the eye, right there from the ground floor. That may not sound like a very bold or ambitious claim to want to make, especially when you consider my subsequent— not to say welcome—involvement in the whole business. Yet I feel privileged to have been there. I feel honored to have, in some small way, *taken part* in that unique, special moment—way back before any of this other complicated cock-and-bull stuff came along. Back when I was a humble grammar book mascot, and Bob T. Hash III, alas now *ante portas,* was just plain old Bob T. Hash III.

The first fledgling phrases of that new eighth edition, I believe, were conceived just a few days after Bob was offered the initial commission. They occurred to him on the Saturday afternoon in the front yard, as he was in the middle of cutting the lawn. From my perch I'd been watching an angst-free Sisyphus (in thick-knit diamond-pattern cardigan) mowing his diagonals like a bishop on a chessboard; when, at a certain point, Bob and his mower came to an unexpected standstill. They stood transfixed in the middle of the lawn, half all neat and crew cut, the other wild and disheveled. The mower's path did not appear to have been halted, however, by a fresh-dug molehill or kamikaze Frisbee.

Moments later, the motor neutralized, Bob sprang into the living room and made a beeline for his work desk. Surely this was not the time to go over the household accounts! ("What's this, Matilda? Parrot feed's gone up again, I see? We're going to have to do something about reining in our collateral expenses") *No, Bob,* I thought to myself, this is not on the schedule. Heedless of this inaudible advice he rummaged about; not a few seconds after, he located both paper and pen. I saw him write something down—*On Saturday afternoons Bob mows the front lawn.*

Within that honest-to-goodness use of the present tense lay the seeds of much greater truths. For Bob, *On Saturday afternoons Bob mows the front lawn* would be—from that moment onward—his Cartesian anchor. With its formulation and commitment to paper, Bob ended several days of doubt, days when he had yet to convince himself whether accepting the commission was the right thing to do. But now he sure knew. He tucked the piece of paper and pen into his pocket and went back to his mowing. From his expression (reposefully smug), and a certain new spring in his step, you could see that in writing that phrase he had made a major decision.

Talking of lawns, one last rather poignant incident. As we know, I came in due course to take over Bob's duties (of which mowing that same lawn was not least). Only last Saturday, in that same diamond-patterned thick-knit cardigan, I myself broke off mid-diagonal not to scribble something down like Bob, but with the altogether more wholesome idea of fetching a beer from the icebox.

Finding the icebox alas empty of beers, I went to look in the cupboard under the stairs. I appear to be still a little unclear as to the correct use of the word *icebox*—but goodness to Betsy, what the Dickens! That cupboard under the stairs gets used as an overflow from the kitchen. I opened the door and turned on the naked 60-watt bulb. Almost immediately, by its harsh white glare, I saw my birdcage and stand. Long time since I'd run across those things! The stand itself was tilted at an angle, on account of the hypotenuse of the stairs. Smaller bits were on a shelf wrapped up in newspaper. You could make out the shape of the rungs on the ladder, and the old-worldly roundness of the mirror. A draft coming up through the floorboards was wafting through the lonely unused bars of the cage.

One day, one day soon, I am going to feel the barrel of a gun jabbing at the small of my back.

Hobbies and Pastimes

Now turn to the page of Everyday Handheld Armaments in the picture book. Student may choose from an Italian Beretta, a silver triggered Stanley, a sprightly Colt 45, a cowboy's wild-western Winchester, and a trumpet-barreled blunderbuss with genuine buckshot . . .

LANGUAGE TIP! Keep out of reach of Bob T. Hash IIIs!

On Friday morning, on the big Friday when the eagerly awaited sales figures from last quarter were going to be announced (around lunchtime), I got Miss Happ to print out my final, crowning modifications. Having checked them over, I declared to myself that the eighth edition of the course book was at last free of meddlesome rampancy and that the last traces of hoax had finally—and forever!—been banished from the republic of Belmont. It was then sealed in the manila and placed in the very out tray where, not all that long ago, I had found it. I straightened my necktie, sighed a team-leading-job-done sigh of relief, and decided to reward myself by taking the afternoon off. On the pretext of fetching something (a stapler) from downstairs, I managed to sidle through the gathering bustle of decorations and slip out of the building unseen. I drove back home where I gorged myself on a whole head of lettuce.

The better to digest my lettuce, I decided to take a siesta. Among vegetables, I believe that lettuce is the least frenzied—but you still have to digest it. There remained one outstanding thing to wrap up this whole business—hands up, yes, Rex?— to return the garden shed to its original time-honored function (its door always bolted to deter an intruder). However, I would take my siesta first, like the hare and the tortoise. Or like Señor Gonzalez. That was what Señor Gonzalez would have done: siesta first, decommission the correctorium mañana (*see—¡Vámonos: Adelante con el Español!*) I had set myself the challenge to salvage the grammar, and having met that challenge, by goodness if I didn't deserve a quick nap!

A bright red cardinal chirped in the shade of a bush when it saw me come out from the back veranda with the intention of digesting my lunch. "Ah, look," I said, pulling a roving garden deck chair into the shade. *"Mon dieu,"* I said, dragging the children's inflatable Michelin-man pool up beside it. The point was to have my feet dangling in the water while I lay in the deck chair. Not without cause I had got the best deck chair available on the postal supermarket (*see* www.GardenDeckchairMonthly .com for some lively online discussion).

Later, as I was dismantling the desk inside the shed après siesta, I suddenly remembered an earth-shattering detail. It concerned the loose-fitting plot around which the course sections hung, and which give the course book its pseudo-biographical shape. Now, toward the end of Bob's bogus version, in token of his own supposedly quiet determination and stalwart profit-stretching service to the institute, Bob T. Hash III, a little too conveniently, was to be posted on a kind of permanent sabbatical.

As I'd progressed through the grammar myself, I'd not only had to prune the grammatical boob-outs of the bogus, but I'd had to make necessary plot adjustments along the way— replacing his rambling picaresque and often contradictory tapestries with the market-driven, primary-key plausibilities of real life. In particular, I did my best to remove any references to his absenting himself and instead had him quietly promoted in the final pages of the course book where, in his new innocuous guise, he would then be at liberty to remain. But, for one reason or another, I'd never actually got round to adjusting this section and in the end I'd simply forgotten all about it. Now go back to section on "Could have done/was going to do."

And now it was still in there, lying snugly in that envelope in the out tray back at the office—Bob still managing to slink off scot-free at the end of the course. To some this might seem a small detail, a mere Hash-ian fly in the ointment. For me it implied not merely a period of forced prolonged exile and further separation from Matilda; it represented a potential breach in the dam through which, if left unrepaired, the whole zany world of Bob T. Hash III might flood back and unravel all my good work.

So, top up on the Plymouth Fury, I rolled back into town to make that final outstanding modification, a Colonel Custard against the Mad Max onflow of traffic commuting home for the weekend. By the time I arrived at Fort Acme, the revelers had long since dispersed. For all intents and purposes (except, say, for producing an utterly unreliable witness or two in any eventual future court trial), the building was empty. When I went through the revolving door, I saw Bert sitting under long sad droops of colorful streamers at the foyer reception desk, like a Duane Hanson installation of a worn-out down-at-the-mouth security guard.

When he saw me, Bert jolted upright. There was a look of troubled surprise on his face, as if he'd just seen a ghost. To cheer him up, I motioned toward the streamers and called out: "Looks like someone's been having a swell party!" I jumped aboard the elevator: *ting* and I was gone.

The open plan section on the top floor was a ghost party of abandoned computer monitors, draped with thin colored strips of festooning party ribbons and anarchic balloons. Here and there a plastic drinking cup with the dregs of a cheap red wine for an ashtray. (*"No, thanks, I don't smoke!"*) As I weaved my way between the partitions, I was puzzling over Bert's double-take expression.

Of course the moment I entered my office, Bert's reaction made complete sense. Bert had looked so surprised to see me coming into the building for the very good reason that he thought I was already inside it, in my fifth-floor executive office. Because there, reinstalled at his one time executive desk, sat none other than Bob T. Hash III in person—calmly browsing through a more than familiar sheaf of typewritten pages, on which I had expended of late a fair chunk of my time.

That Bob had materialized so audaciously in his old office (a streamer/balloon-free enclave) meant he'd got wind of my post-meridian absenteeism, from which he'd deduced that the coast in the office was clear. But the intruder was not the MC meddler or the fumbling hanger-clanging idiot hiding in the wardrobe from a daytime TV sitcom that I'd envisioned finding one day dispensing of dissonant decoction through my files. Bob had somehow gained access to the facilities of bathroom and wardrobe (most probably that excellent en suite installation back on Remington Drive) and was all spruced up in a sharp-looking suit—looking more dapper, more Bob T. Hash III than ever.

Now, willingly and with great alacrity, will I spring forth from behind a discreetly placed foot-dimmer controlled Limbo Arcadia table lamp to point out a grammatical mistake; more than voluntarily will I bounce up from an indolent IKEA Extorp Two Seat Sofa with a Fixed Leather Cover to tick off the unwarranted abuse of syntax—or simply to upbraid the overlong sentence. But however horrendous the mistake, however wayward or persistent the error, I will not swat a fly with a rolled-up copy of the *Belmont Gazette*.

Notwithstanding this aversion to violence (and, I suppose, hoping something might happen in the meantime to avert the need for a showdown in the first place), I had of late found myself entertaining in my mind a number of picture book scenarios by which my rival might meet his doom without requiring my assistance. According to one scenario, I'd pictured a variant of the Asking for Directions situation wherein, disguised in a Bermuda shirt as a foreign tourist (camera round neck), the assassin approaches Bob with a request for directions (to the airport, to the Bristol Hotel?)—only to whip a gun out from his money belt and shoot poor Bob in broad daylight. Another nice idea was a kind of cross between the Everyday Accidents and

Domestic Mishaps section and Lodging a Complaint. An alter-
cation would develop between the bookseller and the client, rising in heat and temper, with the complainant—Bob—coming to
grief beneath a falling stack of books in the somewhat extensive Foreign Language Manual section of the Belmont Barnes
and Noble. I imagined him being challenged to fight a dawn
duel at the edge of the golf course, tethered horses snorting va-
porized plumes into the frosty morning air. I imagined him one
morning getting abducted by the Limbo Martians on the drive
in to work. I imagined him receiving the latest of a long line of
disastrous sales results, pulling a revolver out of a drawer and
shooting himself there at his desk; on the blotting pad, trailing
out from a temple—to some a mere splodge, to others a clotting
Rorschach test of an African gray parrot.

Unfortunately, Bob appeared to have fewer qualms on the
subject of violence than I did. For, when I stepped forward into
the room, my eye was caught by something that looked very
like a large water pistol on the mouse pad—having brazenly
usurped the gray-backed beetle itself—and who knows, it was
quite possibly loaded. Bob may have looked as bland as a Thunderbird, but he sure could turn nasty if things didn't go the way
he'd planned them.

"Ah, there you are," said Bob, looking up, as if this were just
some meeting he'd thrown together in the late afternoon to fi-
nalize some last-minute details of a report. "How good of you to
turn up." Despite his composed air, Bob was unable to stop a
look of unguarded astonishment from flashing across his face—
not so unlike my own reflection on that *Cat in the Hat* day when
I first saw my face in the mirror. Mirrors aside, surgery waiting
rooms aside, neither of us had till this point actually confronted
his doppelgänger at such close quarters; nor had we yet ex-
changed words in our identical voices. Having lived our entire
lives as autonomous beings, we had both simultaneously acquired a fully fledged identical twin who'd managed to turn up
in an identical suit, with an identical haircut and necktie—the

only difference between us being that my twin had come prepared with that little extra military protection.

"I've been having a look through your work here," he said
with a professional tap and an air of self-possession that, rather
worryingly, suggested he *was* several moves ahead after all, being
perhaps abreast of some fact to which I was blind—e.g., his having a wee vial of grammarian's kryptonite in his pocket. When
I heard the man speak, he reminded me of somebody—me.

"You are to be congratulated on a sterling performance."

Flattery would get him nowhere; get him nowhere at all . . .

"However," he went on, his tone subtly changing. "I can't
help noticing a number of things I do not recall having specified
as requiring attention."

As if he'd summoned to his office an applicant copy editor to
whom he would now dispense some indispensable and wise advice that he, the applicant copy editor, would treasure from that
day on till the pinnacle of his professional career, Bob went on
to spin me the story of how he, as president of the Acme International Institute of Languages, had not long ago finished
working on a new edition of the in-house course book called
Forward with English!, that he had been away—only to come
back to find it had suffered such corruptions that it was beyond
recognition. Toying with the pistol on the mouse pad, he asked
me if I had any idea who the perpetrator of these alterations
might be?

I made this shrug and told him I'd only come into the office
to pick up a flip chart, that I wasn't quite sure what he was talking about, and, oh, was there going to be a new eighth edition of
Forward with English!, that's nice, but maybe if he'd seen a flip
chart lying around here I'd be very grateful. I said it was nevertheless an interesting question and that I would let him continue with his work in peace. *Bob felt he should have got that
report done sooner.*

Immune to my request he went on:

"If I might just read you out an example or two of what I'm

getting at," he said, ignoring my polite request for the flip chart. "In my section on Polite Requests my *'He knocked on the door and waited to be admitted'* has become—during my temporary absence—*'he heard a knock on the door and wondered who it could be.'* In my section on the Past Simple, my *'Bob Hash came into the office to make a final adjustment to his* Forward with English! . . .' now reads"—looking up at me with a significant pause—*"he pretended to ask for a flip chart. . . ."*

The odd thing was how *both* the examples of purported errancy he claimed to be reading out and condemning (I was obviously not following his eyes along the page) and his examples of shining melamine rectitude were very much *both* in the same vein as his own purple absurdities—to which I think we have had by now quite ample exposure. There was nothing to distinguish one from the other. In other words, *Bob didn't have a hope of not uttering his gibberish point of view of the world whenever he opened his mouth.* And, needless to say, he was incapable of reading out even a single one of my own sparklingly limpid compositions from the version in front of his nose—from which, thanks to all my hard work, all such above gibberish had been turned into a salted Carthage.

His idea was to lure me in on the joke. Presumably, by making no distinction between the two kinds of sample, between the legit and the ludic, Bob thought he could trap me into proffering some silver-tongued alembication of my own—in the same joshing spirit—so that he could pin the blame on me, and that way bump me off and reclaim his throne.

"What in heaven's name do you think *that* is meant to mean? What the dickens is this?" he said, whacking the manuscript with an avuncular General de Gaullian thump and a mischievous wink. "For all I know, this may be only the tip of the iceberg. By the way, the whole tail is crimson, not just the tip."

He then went on to give me a long list of paired examples, which I shall not repeat here. I had Aphex Twin looping around on my imaginary Walkman.

I will not deny that at moments his raving funambular in-

fractions had an almost infectious joviality, and my face may
now and again have broken into an occasional smile as he "read
out" his examples. "Tut, tut, Mr. Hash," I agreed, wiping a bead
of laughter from my brow, "that does indeed take the cake!—
yes, yes, biscuit in British—Vladimir who?" But, at several
points, when I felt he was removing the water, I also made a
clear show of differing—firmly, with respect—from his tone of
apparent approval. There was a double game going on here.
This man (Bob) was clearly a raving lunatic. But given the
water pistol, I decided it best to tread carefully. At least till I got
the bearings of the situation a little bit more clearly.

To stall for time, I gave Bob a succinct sound-bite-rich eluci-
dation of my own point of view on these matters. I explained
that I myself was a great enthusiast of the Occam's razor approach to the simplification of things in general, how in matters
grammatical I above all else esteemed the clarity flagship pab-
ulum of pig Esperanto Ingleses (imperatives especially I admired for their lack of ambiguity). When Bob then went on to
"cite" further his litany of balderdash (see the apocryphal *Forward with English!*, above), I provided him with helpfully inter-
jected suggestions of how those perversions might stand better
corrected. His wooden dysphasia I checked with the discretion
of a friend. Incursions of the foreign word or phrase provoked in
me the earnest request for a swift and faithful translation,
which I then myself provided (*"Yes, I think the demise of other
languages is a blow to variety too, Jack . . ."*). I pruned his guer-
rilla rum boobies, brushed aside the executive dysfunction and
the hop-skip-and-jump of the melamine prosthesis. There on
the spot I annuled the Gradgrind malarkey, the perturbation of
vernacular pillage (no mercy for either of the double enten-
dres!). I parried the Dionysian dance of the spanner, I neutralized his poetic embellishments, his Gnostic interjections, his
unauthorized ventriloquies, his mongrel macaroni, his homeo-
pathic pre-Acapulcan decoctions, his caravansaries of perver-
sion, his sesquipedalian grandiloquencies, his recreational
Lord Lucansian delinquencies, his asinine assonances, his per-

nicious mescolations, his loose-cannon Wonder-Breadish air-
conditioned genetically modified ethnically cleansed politically
corrected Tourette-syndromish fast-track amphibious frottage.
A final wobbling spoonerism I restored to the upright, like some
empedestaled Ming vase brushed by the hem of a passing
guest's oblivious tail coat that I'd caught and replaced on its
plinth with great tact and cool savoir faire. . . .

"No, no," I said, by way of wrapping up, "that kind of stuff
may in some circles be very amusing, perhaps, but it simply
won't do for the new eighth edition of *Forward with English!* at
all."

Disappointed at his failure to outwit me, Bob leaned back in
my hydraulically sprung-loaded executive chair and scratched
his head (*"No, Miss Scarlett, I must have left them at your
place"*). The dexterity of my defense had dispelled his suspicions
in a trice! So cleverly had I outmaneuvered him at his own
game, so exquisitely timed, so unflustered were my responses
("If I could just pick up that flip chart now, Mr. Hash, and I'll be
off"), that Bob immediately realized that somehow in the
course of his armchair investigations he'd got the wrong end of
the stick. He might rightly try to accuse me of borrowing one of
his suits and demanding a flip chart. Of these I stand guilty as
accused. But it was a long step from those minor offenses to authorship of the hack work in question. Could Bob not have been
"barking up the wrong tree"?

We shook hands, Bob and I. We were the best of pals. Bob
gave me his business card. I had a stack of the things in a
drawer of my desk but I took one anyway. He apologized for his
initial tone of suspicion and hoped I would not hold it against
him. I was a man he could do business with, both today and in
the future. If I saw any signs of the corrupting fiend I should
not hesitate to contact Bob. I looked back at his card . . . *prefix
if you're calling from outside of Belmont.* Sales figures for the
last quarter have been exceptionally good. It was a pity I'd
missed the little party, he said with an imperial sweep of the
arm to the scene beyond the venetians. If I wanted, I could take

a balloon home. "Any color you want." He was under a bit of stress these days. I said I could well understand. I advised him to get some rest, put his feet up. "Take things easy for a bit, Bob," said I, "treat yourself to a vacation," backing this up with a helpful recommendation or two of competitively priced offers on Main Street in Belmont.

Our interview was over. "No need for beefeaters around here," I said, pointing to the three-foot-diameter clock two feet from the front of my nose. I think he appreciated the allusion. It was time I got going. It was time I hit the road. All bonhomie, Bob stood up to accompany his illustrious guest across a swath of plush pile carpet in the direction of egress (the door).

"Oh, don't forget," he announced in a solicitous tone, picking up a fallen flip chart, "your *Golftasche*."

I took it from him and stared at the flip chart.

"Das ist nicht meine Golftasche," I told Bob, holding it out at arm's length with a look of mock consternation on my face. *"Nein, nein. Das ist NICHT meine Golftasche!"*

Courtesies and Polite Requests

In many everyday situations we ask strangers for information or want them to do something for us. Use of the correct form of wording is important when approaching people in order to avoid undue offense.

Examples of "wish": "I wish you wouldn't point that gun at me like that, please."

My momentary and very near fatal slip-up will no doubt remind you of that famous scene in *The Great Escape* with Richard Attenborough and Gordon Jackson in the roles of dapper musicologist and expert in rare Tyrolean musical scores, accompanied by his piano-tuning assistant. Having managed to elude their pursuers through the sleepy Alpine village, they are waiting in line to join traveling villagers (peasant head scarves, baskets of eggs) aboard the little bus that will take them to a glockenspiel convention in a neighboring village nestled among chocolate bar mountains and oblivious cowbells. I too had almost reached freedom, my foot up on the running board of the bus. I too had converted my interrogator's initial suspicions into credulity and a solicitous "good luck" till my gaffe with the *Golftasche*.

"For a moment, for a millisecond . . ." Bob said, motioning me over to a side chair with the barrel of his gun. "Very good. Excellent," he said. "You nearly had me there . . . Mr. . . . Mr. Hash."

Any sense of goodwill there'd been up till then now drained from the room. (My "Come come!" holding up objects to hand— *Is this a book? Is this a pencil?* for example—was not well received.) As I said, Bob could get a bit rattled when things didn't go according to schedule. He snatched back his flip chart. Bob's accusation that it was *I* who'd planted the mangled poppycock errata (of which he of course was the author) was such a preposterous reversal of truth—no, was so outrageous . . . that it was almost impossible to refute. In any case, the loaded pistol advised me against trying to explain that, far from being the prankster, I was the shining knight who had interceded to restore the course book to its pristine condition. There was room in this world for only one Bob T. Hash III. Only one of us was going to leave that room alive. By extension, there was room for only one version of *Forward with English!* And, as things currently stood, the prognosis for my version did not look too brilliant.

Suddenly Bob went left-field. "It appears we have the same taste in suits." He was swiveling about in the comfy executive bucket seat. It was true, we wore identical suits, identical ties, identical glasses, had the same heads and the same vocal intonation. It could be said that Bob was my double. "But I hear our shared tastes extend beyond suits, don't they, Mr. Hash?" (*see* appendix Question Tags, Supplementary Examples). As Bob said this, he reached over the desktop to pick up the framed family photo of the Hashes *en famille,* the one where they're standing on the lawn in front of the veranda and a section of white picket fence. "While I've been away, Mr. Hash, I believe you have been making the acquaintance of my wife? She is hygienic, punctual, and enchanting; she bakes, you'll agree, a most excellent meatloaf."

It was a risk; I had nothing to lose. I proposed Bob a deal. Bob likes doing deals, and so long as I could make it sound like a good one, it might stand a chance. The way things were going at the moment I might not actually see Matilda ever again. The deal, my love for Matilda, *Forward with English!* both now hinged on how well I could sell this deal: it was that or the bullet. Well, I told him, it appears that for one reason or another we both lay claim to the same role, i.e., the much sought-after role of Bob T. Hash III. By the way, she's changed to nut roasts these days. I suggested that execution seemed a tad dramatic as a solution. Perhaps we might come to some better, some more reasonable arrangement? It is not a crime to be half a twin. Nor, as far as I know, is it a crime to find gainful employment on the fifth floor of the Acme International Institute of Languages, and to rise through the ranks like a shining white rein-taker. It is a free country, and Remington Drive has a lot to commend it. The deal is that instead of having just one full-time Mr. Hash, we can have two part-time Mr. Hashes! We can share out duties—at the office, in the coffee shop, at home on weekends. Between us we can effectively halve the workload. "I'm sure Miss Scarlett will be more than happy to sort out some sort of rota, or schedule, for us," I suggested. "Just think of the opportunities to nip off for that extra round of golf." And, in the small matter of which version of *Forward with English!* would get sent to the printers—well, maybe we could come to some kind of gentleman's agreement? I hinted, nudging the air with a sideways jab of an elbow, that if I took care of his wife, he would be left free to elope at will with Miss Scarlett. . . .

"What on earth do you mean by elopement? What in the devil's name are you talking about?" he interrupted, with uncharacteristic vehemence. "I have been away on an extended business trip and Miss Scarlett has been injured in a skiing accident."

And it was true, dear student, Bob had only been away on a business trip, and Miss Scarlett had only been injured on a ski trip. When from the conference foyer Bob had called in to the office, I had been the one to answer the phone, and when doing so I had resorted to my parrot's imitatory powers to assure him, in the voice of a reliable colleague, that the office was running like clockwork: "Sure," I said. "So quiet here in the office, you could hear a pin drop, or a brick of asbestos, so you might as well stay on to take advantage of that special offer on at the spa facilities after all. . . ." And when Miss Scarlett, lying in her hospital bed with her leg set in plaster, had called with the sad news of her thigh, I had reassured her—in the voice of Bob himself—that the backlog was well under control: "No need to rush back here, Miss Scarlett. Get thee well soon" (*see* Thee vs. Thou). In reality, Bob had been away on an extended business trip and from it had now inevitably returned as if he'd been attached by a very long elastic band that had sort of twanged him back in when the elastic contracted.

I'm going to speculate a bit here on how things might have gone on Bob's return from his business trip. From a short, quite puzzling conversation with his wife that morning as he took off his coat in the hall, Bob rapidly gleaned two salient and terrible facts: that his wife was having an affair, and that the person she was having it with was his identikit double. Fearing instinctively for his precious *Forward with English!* he had put on his coat again and with the armament of his choice rushed to the office to check on his out tray. His premonition in the line at the airport regarding his parrot was alas coming true. And, regarding Miss Scarlett, he must have learned about the skiing injury from her hospital postcard lying on the desk. My much better version of *Forward with English!* (eighth edition) that he held now on his desk was the one missing piece of the jigsaw puzzle he'd needed to tie up the picture. (Had my interview with Miss Ratcliffe, had my phone call with the printer, had that article in the *Belmont Gazette,* had Miss Scarlett's voice mail itself, only been figments of my imagination? Pah!)

No wonder my suggestion went down like a down-moving thing. Despite the prospect of all that extra golf my offer of compromise was rejected. Greedy Bob would give up neither Miss Scarlett nor his *Forward with English!* without a fight to the death.

How easily—if Bob's version of events were true, how easily might I then have been subtracted from the scene and nobody been one whit the wiser. From an evolutionary or biodiversical point of view I was merely a parrot. Parrots fly through windows and go live in the local parks. With what impunity I—the nonexistent, the deceased parrot, the carbon copy, my Gordon Jackson smartly brogued Boswellian foot still tap tap tapping up on the running board of the little coach—could be liquidated and forgotten.

At this point a puppeteer's invisible wire and harness arrangement made me edge backward, dragging my Hush Puppies along the carpet, like there were a magnet in my back. The word in English is "stagger." Presently, one puppet string pulled on my jaw and made me say, "No, Bob"—fairly disingenuously— "I don't think I need that flip chart after all. Come to think of it, we'll just use the overhead projector."

"Not so fast, my dear Mr. Hash"—sibilating on the last word like a thespian priest. "We are not quite finished yet. We are forgetting about our course book. By the way, the overhead projector is in room 508. Miss Slowcomb was using it for her talk on motivational strategies this morning."

Here is the scene where the mad scientist, thwarted at the last moment from blowing up the world, in turn unmasks and disarms his thwartee—just in time to see his original plan through: so sit back and relax. There could well be a car chase or an underground lair with bleeping computers and a white-tailed shark in a pool. Well, in any case, from the faded leather battered briefcase with a bashed-out clasp that had been lurking at his feet, Bob took out—no, not the famous pre-Columbian copy of the primer thought lost to the mists of time but his own whacked-out version, a photocopy that he must have kept with him for posterity's sake and which thus, like a phoenix, had survived the barbecue embers. This he laid with a small thud beside the sheaf already lying there on the desktop. Student, Rex, please now take note: *two identical sheaves of paper side by side—identical twins ruling their fate.*

"I think the printer has been waiting for this—and should be rewarded for his patience," announced Bob (tapping one or the other of the sheaves, forgetting, already, which one was which).

"My *Chèr Herr Caro Signor Señor Pan,* my dear Mr. Hash," Bob continued, getting up at last from the desk, "take a seat. Your desk"—giving the chair a triumphant shock-absorbed swivel—"is now free!"

"We shall have you commit suicide, said he with a flourishing bow. This will boost sales of our latter-day primer! 'Sympa-

thy sales' is the technical term. *No, you cannot phone the suicide hotline just now. They'll be busy.* Please listen carefully. I'm
going to have two households to run now, you understand. Who
knows, maybe some more mouths to feed in the future. An impostor Mr. Hash will have shot himself in his office. Oh, I don't
know why. Tragic sales figures, personal problems, looking like
Bob T. Hash does; the reason's not important. The important
thing is our little primer, my little primer, will be safe. It will
sell like hotcakes, Mr. Hash, rest assured. Our nice bland *Forward with English!*

"Such a pity we're not going to have time for that round of
golf," he said, checking me with a flick of the barrel. "Unless,
that is," he taunted, "your clubs make it here in time from their
round-the-world tour . . ."

Bob's own fatal, landmarking mistake was his insane attempt to dispense with my *Forward with English!* prior to taking
care of his enemy and rival—what some might call an example
of hubris. I was keeping a parrot's eye on those sheaves, to
make sure there were no sleights of hand. I saw him pick up *the
wrong sheaf.* Instead of my nice bowdlerized *Forward with English!* he had picked up the only surviving copy of his own bogus
version. Being a humane kind of plot merchant, Bob wanted me
to exit this world with the indelible understanding that his was
the version of *Forward with English!* that would triumph and
that my attempt to save the course book had failed. "No need
to worry, you also-ran," he said, tapping the (mistaken) manuscript. "I'll make sure the right version reaches the printers.
Just leave that up to me." I almost felt sorry for the poor chap.

With that, already *in piedi,* Bob started backing away from
me (also *in piedi*), reversing toward the back window, the wrong
sheaf of paper in his free left hand, the gun in the other, the
right, trained on the author of this sentence—the idea being to
kill the sheaf first by ditching it out of the window. Only then to
kill me . . . *No, Bob, I'm afraid the shredder's still out of order.*

What Bob wasn't aware of, however, apart from the fact he
wasn't holding the version of *Forward with English!* that he

thought he was holding, was that during his absence (Acapulco/ extended business conference?) the office windows had undergone something of a *Verwandlung* themselves. A team of glaziers had been called in to replace the old-style windows, grown rusty and stiff with age (quite possibly not replaced since the era of Mr. Cotton). The old windows, which had swiveled on a horizontal axis, had been replaced with a new kind of window, which swiveled on a vertical axis instead. So, when Bob came to give the window the proverbial good old shove (as he would have done with the old stiff framed ones), there was a sudden, unexpected give and a consequent rather dramatic loss of footing. . . .

Active vs. Passive
(*proficiency-level students only*)

E xamples:

- *A banana skin was placed near the window. (passive)*
- *The clitoris was discovered by Renaldus Columbus in 1559. (passive; remote past)*
- *The course book has been corrected and is now safe for consumption. (passive)*
- *He slipped and fell out the window. (active)*

The impression of Bob that will stick most in my mind is much like the one from the Everyday Accidents and Domestic Mishaps section in the picture book, where he slips on an icy sidewalk on the way to the post office—necktie over his shoulder astream in the updraft, his startled eyeglasses jumping off the bridge of his nose, his legs backpedaling in midair—except in the current case he's a lot higher up from those bone-smashing flagstones. And, during that short slapstick flight before he crumpled like a pack of cards, you can imagine passing through Bob's mind a number of vignetted scenes from his picture book past, the way ex-drownees say a drowner's life will pass before him as he's drowning, or as she is—in a whirling dervish of Scheherazadian images: the still life of a breakfast table (an apple gleaming in sunlight; a Vermeerian milk jug; the window of clear dear blue sky reflected in the convexity of his cereal spoon); buying a cranberry-and-bronze necktie at the department store; sharing the children's trampoline on the weekend with three-feet diameter, tumbling terpsichorean clock faces; and inevitably packing his business-trip suitcase. like a Sideshow Bob teetering at the top of Wittgenstein's ladder, doffing his trilby in a final farewell to the milliner's wife . . . *Breath of fresh air will do you the world of good, Bob.*

   Still in shock, and without further descriptive ado (it hadn't helped that there was a banana skin on the floor under the window either) I dashed across to the window to see how I might be of assistance—a bit optimistic, that, I suppose— half dreading the possibility he'd be twitching like a botched slaughtered pig or a crash-test dummy phantom limb in the oblivion below.

Luckily, Bob had not fallen on the concrete flagstones at all. Yet, equally fatally, he had fallen like a sack of Irish potatoes (now, there's a "moving-down thing" if we need one again) clean into one of the big recycle drums, whose lid, by the force of impact, had conveniently flipped shut behind him. By virtue of his weight he had reached the ground first. But the white sheets of foolscap on which the one extant copy of his own babbling compositions was in print were still for the most part making their descent, seesawing down through the air, like at the ticker tape parades for a returning cavalcade of astronauts. All would get turned into mush.

Under pressure, in moments of crisis, as cool as a cucumber, I can be as brisk as a honky-tonk piano. Assured by the total quietness coming from the bin that Bob was 100 percent dead, deceased, ex, etc., like that parrot in Monty Python, I went back to the desk where my own bowdlerized version lay. (This is the bit near the end of the episode of *Commissioner Rex* where, clutched between his canines, paws up on the desk, the eponymous tail-wagging Rex would bring me the correct and rescued version of *Forward with English!*) With my trusty Parker, I made the written adjustments (a last crowning nip and tuck) that would keep course book Bob installed at that desk: the last little amendment that I'd come to the office to make. I put the pages inside the manila envelope, checked the address, and settled it for posting in my out tray with Zen-like precision.

Next thing (*"Oops, a bit drafty there. Would you mind if I closed the window?"*), I was striding through the maze of eerie partitions and abandoned desks in the direction of the lift shafts. There was not a great deal of time to make a big list of things I'd noticed along the way to tell you about, but I did at least have time for two: a phone with tinsel wrapped round it, which rang three times and then fell silent; and a photocopier that someone had forgotten to switch off—a tiny light flashing to show a helpless sheet of paper had been mangled in its rollers. Well did *I* know that flashing pinpoint of light.

At the lifts, I encountered an ill-paid, unmotivated cleaning lady with again a Duane Hanson look of bedraggled exhaustion, wringing out a string-wig floor mop that reeked of disinfectant. The cleaner can't have recognized me, otherwise she'd have gone *Nighty night, Mr. Hash. Have a good weekend. You just put your feet up now. You deserve it, Mr. Hash!* On the spur of the moment, and in a spirit of magnanimous generosity, I offered the cleaning lady a (pre-payable) course of discounted language instruction as dispensed by upstanding pedagogue, etc.—or at least that's what I *tried* to offer her. Not speaking English, she did not understand me and there was hardly time for me to go into all the ins and outs of my offer very slowly. And, in any case, I had just used up my remaining resource of mental patience by observing the bleeping photocopier and that symbiotic tinsel phone.

It didn't really matter though. With the new unblemished eighth edition of *Forward with English!* at last ready for the printer, the last threat to its safe expedition now removed, my career as troubleshooter had effectively come abruptly to a halt. I did not have to give the lady lessons to keep the wolf from the door. From an editorial point of view, my services as a supply Bob were no longer required either. If I so wished, I could simply drive out of picture book Belmont and shack up with Matilda in a hippie camper somewhere in the Nevada desert— secure in the knowledge that *Forward with English!* was safe and out in the Belmont Barnes and Noble.

But apart from any invaluable involvement in the course book's composition, being Bob T. Hash III and thus Matilda's good husband was a role I'd indeed grown to like. "Yes," I said, in my imitation screechy parrot voice when I was back inside the lift and no one could hear me (except for that little microphone in the corner), "I quite like being Lord Macbeth, Bob, I dare say"—in a bluegrass accent out of the blue. Yes. There was more to life than power-correcting a scrambled-up language course after all!

My labors on the course book were now over. My humbler day's duties in the office were now done. It was time to return to Remington Drive and the Friday night nut roast.

Brush Up On:
Places to Wave From

Examples: at the quayside, on the railway station platform, at the departure lounge of Belmont International Airport.

—Matilda was waving at Bob from the veranda.
—Bob waved back from the car.

Now read the dialogue and answer the following question:

Which Bob T. Hash III waved back from the car as it cruised up Remington Drive?

Discuss in class.

To round this all up then, I think we'd agree on one thing at least. We'd agree that, generally speaking, I have put my metamorphosis to the good. Other parrots finding themselves turned into a Bob T. Hash III might have had a right old time stirring things up: vertiginous cribbings, voice hoaxes left, right, and center—the pick of the stenographer pool . . . (*Hey, hang on a minute, wasn't there something back there about parrots being monogamous?*) . . . not to mention the additional fun and games they too—like Bob— might have had with the new eighth edition of *Forward with English!*

"Thanks, Bob, we appreciate the work you did on the new edition of Forward with English!*—it's awesome!"* But by no one are my efforts going to be more appreciated, more welcome than by Matilda, my wife.

Imbued, therefore, with a great sense of Zen-like equanimity (re: the manila envelope, for example) regarding the present and with optimistic Olympian-like visions for the future, I steered the Plymouth Fury homeward, top down, with warm evening air once more swishing gracefully through my hair like an advertisement for the banishment of dandruff. And now that the business with the dodgy course stuff was done with, I knew the one thing left to do was to tell Matilda what had become of her parrot. With Bob dead and the primer back in the weekend out tray I knew also that the time to tell her was now at last come.

I was thinking about all this, how strange and marvelous a story it all was when, halfway along Remington Drive in my electric milk cart, I caught sight of Matilda. She was outside the house waving at me from the veranda.

84

Advanced Certificate
*further possible ways by which you might
have infiltrated the picture book world
of the course book*

a) You are an incorrigible African gray parrot with a crimson-tipped tail. Through a casual discovery, the main protagonist of the language course book discovers he is able to "Jekyll-and-Hyde" himself into your doppelgänger parrot, and as such has been trying to dislodge you from your perch—with the intention of usurping your position as domestic pet in the picture book protagonist's house, thus mascot to the primer. One of the twin parrots now appears to lie dead at the base of the bird stand. The aim here is to prove that you, as opposed to the dead body underneath the bird stand, are the real and original Comenius, favorite son of Belmont.

b) Besides being the author and illustrator of the language course book, you suffer from an extremely rare medical condition whereby you sometimes enter a coma so profound that it is virtually impossible to distinguish it from mortal demise. Such an episode has just occurred and you are now in the deepest of comas where, though dead to the outside world (but still under pressure of a very real publishing deadline), you continue to work on the gobbledygook grammar book scenarios in your comatose dreamscape.

c) Bamboozled by relentless marketing pressures, you have parted with a vast sum of the local currency for what turns out to be a shoddy half-baked but immaculately presented course in foreign language instruction. You are now overidentifying with the picture book characters and the stories around them to the point where you are no longer able to distinguish between your own reality and that of the picture book. In a fit of paranoid delusion you decide that the only way to remain in the picture book is to push the tycoon protagonist and his golf bag out a window.

d) Rather than it being you inside the grammar book, it is in fact the grammar book that has got inside of you. An irrepressible babble of voices from within prompts you to speech pattern distortions, the substitution of perfectly good English terms and phrases with unwarranted foreign translations, and the po-faced elaboration of red herring subplots.

e) (*variant of possibility* a *in First Steps*) With your favorite tweed-upholstered armchair drawn up to a glowing hearth side, you are in the upstairs library of your country residence. Puffing away on your pipe, you chortle over a vellum-bound volume of *Alice's Adventures in Wonderland* resting merrily in your lap. Suddenly, not far from the beginning, a phrase concerning a long-eared bobtailed furry rodent mammal of the Leporidae family famed for its predilection for gregarious breeding that burrows under golf courses and is delicious with onions sends you urgently padding over in your carpet slippers to an alcoved set of candlelit polyglot bookshelves to follow up on the reference. On removal of *The Observer Book of Rabbits White* from its perch (as from a hat), the bookshelf unit swivels inward to reveal a secret torch-lit passageway connecting at length with Mr. Hash's executive office (emerging from the office filing cabinet, section N–Z).

f) You have actually always been in the picture book. No explanation is therefore required.

Now write a novel that you might like to anchor in one or in some combination of the above scenarios (student may also use scenarios from First Steps) that, by giving grammatical guidance, illustrative examples, student exercises, etc., might not only provide an entertaining read but prove useful as teaching material in its own right for the benefit of class.

About the Author

DAVID DEANS was born and raised in Edinburgh, Scotland, and educated at the University of Aberdeen and the London School of Economics. He has spent many years abroad teaching English as a second language and currently lives in Italy.

About the Type

This book was set in Century Schoolbook, a member of the Century family of typefaces. It was designed in the 1890s by Theodore Low DeVinne of the American Type Founders Company, in collaboration with Linn Boyd Benton. It was one of the earliest types designed for a specific purpose: the *Century* magazine, maintaining the economies of a narrower typeface while using stronger serifs and thickened verticals.